Unforeseen

by K.G. Croston

Hope you enjoy!

K. G. Croston

Bolt Publishing, LLC

An Orlando based publishing company

Copyright 2021 by K.G. Croston

1 9 2 8 3 7 4 6 5

Publisher Note:

This book is a work of fiction.
All of the names, places,
and events that occur are from
the author's imagination.
Any resemblance to an actual
person, alive or dead, place,
historical event, or business establishment
is purely coincidental.

Contributions:

Editorial Team:
Lead Editor – JA Lafrance
Content and Story – Stephanie Croston

Cover Design – Jeremy Croston
Social Media and Web Design – Ryan Latterell

More from K.G. Croston!

Kidnapped

Mystery at Sleepy Hollow: Ride On

Return to Sleepy Hollow

Mystery at O'Gill's Vineyard

Mystery at Maple Tree Inn

Table of Contents

More from K.G. Croston!   3

Table of Contents   4

Dedication   5

Chapter 1   6

Chapter 2   21

Chapter 3   30

Chapter 4   45

Chapter 5   56

Chapter 6   69

Chapter 7   84

Chapter 8   98

Chapter 9   110

Chapter 10   122

Chapter 11   138

Chapter 12   149

Dedication

This book is dedicated to Biscuit, Hunter and JJ. Until our paths meet again...

Chapter 1

It's hard to believe that it's been a year since Katelyn Winters and her sister, Abby attended a murder mystery weekend at Winchester Estate. Katelyn is a writer and received an invitation to the event, and Abby invited herself along. It was supposed to be an enjoyable get-a-way at the beautiful estate and Katelyn was hoping to meet some of the other authors in her group. A few of them lived in or visited other countries and had hectic schedules making the travel impossible at times. The make-believe crime scene would give them all a chance to work together to figure out 'who done it.' Unfortunately, a real mystery took place that involved a kidnapping. Katelyn shuddered every time she thought of it. Katelyn and Abby went home with several new friends.

The news media covered the story of the murder mystery events, and Katelyn and Abby were immediately thrown into the spotlight. Abby loved the attention and was more than happy to speak to them. She did a few live broadcasts and the audience fell in love with her. She sort of became a local celebrity while Katelyn preferred to stay out of the limelight. Abby was offered a position at the local news station where she reported on various events and did special news reports throughout the county. Katelyn went back to her writing and was working on a new mystery taking place in Virginia, a state she fell in love with mainly due to its colonial atmosphere.

Mystery writer, Katelyn Winters, was getting ready to go out for a run around her neighborhood. She lived on Westbrook Lane in Bedford Falls, Massachusetts. Her dog, Biscuit, was napping in her bedroom upstairs. They had been to the dog park earlier, and Biscuit was most likely tired from chasing her friend, a Bichon Frise named Peaches, around the park. Her owner, Sandy, was a good friend of Katelyn's and they met there quite often to catch up while their dogs played. Just as Katelyn was putting in her earbuds, her cell phone rang. She didn't recognize the number and decided to answer with her normal business greeting.

"Hello, this is Katelyn Winters."

"Hi Katelyn, it's Ellen Stratford."

Ellen is a writer that Katelyn befriended at an author event a couple of years ago. She had been writing mysteries for over twenty years and is from Kansas City. They became closer last year when they were tossed into their own mysterious series of events at Winchester Estate.

"Katelyn, what did you decide about this year's mystery cruise?"

Katelyn didn't have a clue what she was talking about but then she looked at the huge stack of unopened mail piled up on her desk. She saw a large packet that she thought was junk mail when it was delivered. "A mystery cruise? Wow, that sounds like a lot of fun." Katelyn opened the packet and sure enough, it was her invitation.

"Yep, I got it. Did you have a chance to look over the information?"

"Yes, I did. Dear, the registration deadline is today so if you're going you have to decide rather quickly."

"I'm so glad you called. I'll get started looking over the information right away."

"Good and in the meantime, I'll contact Donovan, William, Amber, and Weldon and arrange a zoom call for all of us."

"That would be great, Ellen! Let me know when, as I'm anxious to catch up with everyone."

"Sounds good. Talk to you soon."

After Katelyn hung up, she was more interested in reading the information in the packet than going out for her run. She ran up and down her front steps a few times thinking that would count toward her exercise goal for the day. She opened the front door, and Biscuit was waiting for her to come inside.

"Hey girl, did you get some rest after your busy morning?"

Biscuit walked over and stood in front of the cabinet where her dog treats were stored. Katelyn had to laugh as she grabbed a bone for her to snack on. She made herself a glass of iced tea and went into the living room. She opened the packet, and as soon as she had everything spread out, the doorbell rang. She got up to answer it and saw it was her sister, Abby.

"Hey Abby, I wasn't expecting you."

"Thanks for the warm welcome. I didn't know I needed to call and request an appointment to see you." Abby can be so dramatic, Katelyn thought.

"Oh, I didn't mean it that way. I was on my way out when Ellen Stratford called."

"How's Ellen doing? It seems like forever since we saw her at the Winchester Estate."

"She's doing fine. She was calling to see if I received an invitation to the mystery cruise in the…"

"What? Did you say a mystery cruise?" Abby interrupted, and instead of keeping her in suspense, Katelyn showed her the information displayed on her coffee table.

"Wow – this is great!" The promotional ad read: 'This year's murder mystery cruise will take place while sailing through the Bermuda Triangle!' "That sounds fantastic! We have to go!"

"We? Since when are you a mystery writer?" Katelyn asked jokingly.

Abby rolled her eyes and asked, "Do you think Donovan and William will be there? I hope so."

"Well, I'll find out on the zoom call Ellen's setting up."

"When is it? I have to be on it too!" Abby said excitedly, ignoring Katelyn's remark.

"Well, after she gets in touch with them, Weldon and Amber, she'll let me know. In the meantime, I think we need to review the material and see if we can make it."

"Are you serious?" Abby asked with her right hand positioned on her hip. "Of course, we can make it!"

They sat down on the sofa and began to read the details. "Oh my gosh, Katelyn, the cruise is in six weeks!"

"Whoa…that's soon? It doesn't give us much time. Besides, your job may not appreciate the short notice and I have to see if I can get Biscuit a reservation at Puppy Trails."

Abby did another one of her famous eye rolls and stopped listening to her. "Do you always have to be so gloomy? Look on the bright side for a change."

"Okay, before we get too carried away, why don't you check with your boss and see if you can get some time off. In the meantime, I'll call Gabriela and see about getting Biscuit taken care of."

After Katelyn made her call, she was glad Biscuit was able to get her one of their deluxe suites. She loved Biscuit and always felt bad when she had to leave her behind.

However, the staff at Puppy Trails always said that she seemed to enjoy her visits and playing with the other dogs.

She went into the kitchen to get Abby a glass of iced tea and make some sandwiches when Abby's cell rang. She overheard Abby trying to sell her boss on the idea of sending her on this cruise as an assignment.

"Uh-huh, I understand. Yes, of course, I'm sure there'll be lots of activities to report on that would be of interest to our viewers as well as interviews with a few of the authors. I'm looking at the itinerary now. We are scheduled to travel through the Bermuda Triangle."

That must have been the selling point that Abby made with her boss. "Yes, of course, I'll be able to handle this assignment. Besides, I met a lot of the mystery writers last year so I'll have plenty of human interest stories. Uh-huh, great, I'll email you all of the details. We have a zoom call scheduled with some of the authors so I can go over my news reporting with them. Sounds good, talk to you soon."

After she hung up, she took a large sip of her iced tea and said, "Guess who's not using vacation or paying for their trip, sister?"

Katelyn laughed. "You always find an angle, don't you? What kind of news reporting are you going to subject our friends to? Better yet, don't tell me."

"There's going to be an escape room excursion! How fun is that!" Abby continued reading the itinerary and was thinking about what she would need to take when Ellen called Katelyn back. She could hear Abby in the background and asked, "Is it safe to assume that Abby's joining us on the cruise?"

"You didn't think otherwise, did you?" Katelyn teased.

"No, I would be disappointed if she didn't. I contacted the others and scheduled our call for seven this evening. I'm emailing everyone the call information now."

"Great, we'll go ahead and send in our registration and look forward to talking to everyone later."

After Ellen hung up, she limped over to her chair. She had just made a cup of tea to go along with her scone. She was worried that her condition wouldn't be better in time for the cruise.

Unknown to her, a figure stood outside her living room window and was watching her every move.

As she sat down, she thought she heard a noise outside, but when she looked, she saw nothing. Must have been a tree branch blowing in the wind or one of the squirrels that ran up and down the tree looking for acorns, she thought. The figure stayed still for a little while to make sure Ellen didn't see them before swiftly walking into the neighbor's yard behind her house.

At seven sharp, Abby was already dialed in for the call. Katelyn hurriedly ran from her office with pen and paper in hand.

"Hello everyone," Ellen greeted. One by one, everyone joined in and was interested in what everyone else had been doing since last year's event.

William had been in Ireland researching his next mystery. It was taking place in a remote village in the picturesque countryside. He was exploring the castles and doing some research on the area. He had just returned to his home in London. Donovan was enjoying some time off in the south of France. He was traveling to various cities and taking his time on writing his next book.

Katelyn and Abby, along with the others were surprised to hear that Weldon and Amber were collaborating on a book together. After last year's event, it seemed they grew closer and everyone was glad they mended their differences and started a friendship.

"What's your book about?" William asked.

"Well, I can assure you it's more interesting than a castle stuck out in the middle of nowhere in Ireland!" Weldon remarked.

"Katelyn dear, what have you been doing with yourself?" Ellen quickly asked changing the subject.

Before she could answer, Abby, burst out, "Absolutely nothing!"

"Really, Abby, you know that's not true!"

Katelyn was in a slump after her breakup with Officer Ryan, but it was amicable and they never really did get serious. He hated hurting her feelings, but an old girlfriend from his college days contacted him. What was supposed to be a catch-up dinner turned out to be more dates, and then they decided to give their relationship another try. Katelyn understood but she occasionally wondered 'what if' she never showed up.

Abby, on the other hand, was too busy to worry about Officer York leaving town since her career took off and she had more assignments than she could handle. Luckily, Katelyn wasn't the jealous type and never minded her sister's celebrity status in town. However, it could get annoying when they were out having lunch or dinner, and people would come up and ask for her autograph. Abby always introduced her, and occasionally, people would ask Katelyn for her signature as well.

They found it interesting that Donovan met a French woman while he was on his trip and invited her to join him on the cruise. William, on the other hand, was still content with the bachelor lifestyle. "So, what is your mademoiselle's name?" Amber asked.

"It's Brigitte, and before you ask, she has a small café, and I met her when I was..."

"No one cares about your love life..."

"Weldon, that's enough!" Amber said it in such a way that it shocked everyone, especially Weldon who didn't get a chance to finish his sentence.

Everyone could tell he was embarrassed by Amber's outburst and said, "Well, now that we're caught up on everyone's boring lives, let's get down to business, shall we?"

Unfortunately, it seemed that his old habits had resurfaced, which included being annoying. He did have a way with spoken and written words.

"Of course, let's get started," Ellen added.

She knew how to handle Weldon and began with the first day's itinerary. Everyone agreed to meet at the ship at noon when registration began and lunch was to be served in the Stowaway dining room. Later that day at four o'clock, the ship would begin its voyage, and everyone agreed to gather on the deck with the others attending the cruise from their mystery writers' organization. They found it interesting that there was a total of five groups of mystery writers attending. Even though they didn't have any friends or loved ones showing up to wish them a bon voyage, it was a ship's tradition to wave to those seeing them off from the dock. Of course, a drill was scheduled at three o'clock where everyone on board would meet at pre-arranged locations to go over the emergency procedures while on board. Everyone needed to attend, and once that was over, the guests were ready to party to a live band on the Aloha deck.

"This sounds like so much fun!" Abby said as she jumped up from the sofa.

"I see your enthusiasm is still running at a level of 'out of control'", Weldon lamented. "What's your officer boyfriend think of your newfound fame?"

Upon hearing that, Abby quieted down and let the others speak.

The first day was a sea day. The activities included a gathering of the hosts and all of the author groups after breakfast. Then, a luncheon was being held in the Captain's dining room, followed by a Meet and Greet with the Sea Voyage Club guests. These were the folks that sailed on ten or more sailings and were given a special meeting with the authors for short book readings, Q&A, book signings, and for the authors to fill them in on future book releases. Usually, many of these VIP guests were fans of various writers.

Everyone agreed to have their book orders delivered directly to the ship, as recommended by the cruise line. They were hoping to attract new readers and sell out of as many books as possible. Weldon chuckled and Amber asked, "What's so funny, old man?"

"I was just thinking about the last book you wrote on your own."

Amber wasn't appreciative of his comment. The last book she wrote before joining forces with him was a disaster. Her publisher threatened to take away her current book deal. Lucky for Amber, her publisher was also working with Weldon on his books, and word got back to him about her dilemma. Since he was a good friend of her father's, he couldn't let her go down like this. Even though her father had a few unpublished books she could benefit from, he didn't want her to deceive anyone by using them as her own. If they were published, they should be under her father's name.

"Okay then, moving on, let's take a look at the second day's agenda." Katelyn hadn't said much but the bantering back and forth was giving her a headache. They reviewed each day's scheduled activities and decided on a few excursions they would like to sign up for. Of course, just about everyone was interested in the escape room. Ellen secretly worried about her recent injury as it may prove to be too much for her.

"I see we'll be traveling through the Bermuda Triangle on day four, followed by the main event we're all waiting for; the disappearance of ..." Katelyn was cut off by one of the guys making a scary laugh. She was finally excited about something and began telling the others about her readings on the mysterious disappearance of folks either on ships or planes when going through the Bermuda Triangle.

"Katelyn, that's hogwash. Nothing has ever been proven that the Bermuda Triangle was responsible for any of their disappearances." Weldon probably did some research on the subject as well but he always came across as a wise guy, Amber thought.

"Well, let's get packed, folks! We only have six short weeks until we set sail." Donovan was anxious to get off the call and was getting ready to call Brigitte. Everyone said their goodbyes and decided to check in with each other the following week.

After they hung up, Abby showed her displeasure in Weldon's behavior. "Katelyn, do you believe Weldon? I thought he changed!"

"Well, maybe he's not feeling well or under a lot of stress right now."

"Yeah, probably stressed out trying to write a book with Amber. Do you believe they teamed up?"

"To tell you the truth, Abby, I think there's more to the story. But regardless, it's none of our business."

They finished completing their online registration and made plans to go shopping the next evening. After Abby left, Katelyn walked into her closet to see if she had any appropriate cruise attire. Unfortunately, most of her clothing was suited for colder weather, and she didn't care for the out-of-style summer clothes she had. Besides, she knew Abby was always making a fashion statement since getting her new job and was sure the others would also be well dressed.

After glancing through her emails, she saw one from Amber that was sent to everyone on the call except for Weldon and of course, Abby. As she read it, she realized what had been going on between her and Weldon. It read:

Friends, please accept my apology for my inappropriate comments made to Weldon this evening. I think he has gotten worse lately, and usually, when we are working together, I can tolerate him. Other days, I could just kill him. I just wanted to let you know so you are all aware since we'll be on the mystery cruise together in a few weeks.

Talk to you soon!

-Amber

After Katelyn finished reading it, Ellen called. She figured something was up with Weldon, and while discussing their zoom call conversation, a lone figure was standing in front of her living room window staring directly at her. This time, Ellen noticed and quietly said to Katelyn, "There's someone outside my window looking in at me!"

Katelyn gasped and asked if she wanted her to stay on the line and use her landline to call the police. Ellen agreed and gave her the address. The police said they would have a patrol car there in less than five minutes.

Ellen tried to stay calm and continued her conversation with Katelyn. She told her in hushed tones that she couldn't see the individual and wasn't sure why anyone would be stalking her. "I just wish the police would get here soon." Katelyn was worried and knew Ellen lived alone and didn't have any close relatives.

Just as soon as the patrol car parked in front of Ellen's neighbor's house, the person standing outside took off. The police officer walked around the perimeter of her house and didn't see anyone. He knocked on the door and showed Ellen his identification. His name was Officer Bradford. She invited him inside and he asked her about her injury. Katelyn was still on the line and overheard the officer. As soon as he made that remark, Ellen thanked Katelyn for her help and hung up. She didn't want Katelyn to know about her accident.

"Ma'am, I walked around outside and didn't see anyone."

"Yes, officer, the person must have seen your car, and immediately ran off."

He asked her the normal routine questions and began to fill out the report. "I will keep an eye out this evening as I patrol your neighborhood."

He told her to make sure all of her doors and windows were locked and secured before he found his way out. He made another trip around the yard before leaving. Ellen slowly made her way upstairs to her bedroom which she was glad was on the second floor. She normally hated using the staircase with her cane and aching legs and feet, but tonight she felt safer being upstairs, and hopefully, away from prying eyes. She was glad she invested in a security system just in case someone tried to enter her home. Once in her bedroom, she texted Katelyn to let her know that she was okay and was getting ready to go to bed. She knew it was going to be a long, restless night.

***

After Katelyn received her text, she filled Abby in on Ellen's mysterious visitor. "Do you think Ellen is seriously being stalked?"

"I don't know, but Ellen was scared out of her mind. She must have done something to herself since I overheard the officer ask her about an injury."

"That's strange, I wonder what happened, and if she'll be okay in time for the cruise."

"Well, I'll call her tomorrow to check up on her and maybe she'll let me know."

"Okay, see you tomorrow and you can fill me in on what you find out."

***

Donovan was anxiously waiting for Brigitte to call. He phoned earlier but she said she was busy at the café and would call him back. He was surprised as she usually anticipated his evening calls and the café was closed. She was typically there when the crew did the cleanup, and usually started prepping the food for the next day. It was getting late so he tried calling her again.

This time instead of going straight to voicemail, a man speaking French answered groggily, "Bonjour." Donovan was taken aback and asked to speak to Brigitte.

"Qui est-tu?" the man asked.

Donovan knew he was asking who he was, and instead of answering him, Donovan replied by asking him who he was. At this point, the phone was answered by Brigitte.

"Bonjour Donovan!"

"Bonjour ma Chère!" Donovan answered back. "Who was the man who answered your phone?"

"Ah, Donovan, that was Jacques, he was assisting me with my pastries for tomorrow."

He loved hearing her French accent.

"It sounded like he was sleeping and I woke him up."

She laughed, "Oh no, an employee sleeping while at work. Off with his head," she joked.

Donovan was confused and wondered why she was still working at the café. "Donovan, I have pastries to take out of the oven. I will call you back when I wake up tomorrow. Okay, mon Chère?"

"Okay, ma Chère."

***

At seven o'clock the next morning, Ellen heard a knock on her front door. She peeked outside the windows before asking who was there. "Ma'am, it's Officer Bradford. I'm just checking in on you."

"Okay, please come in," Ellen answered.

"I'm going off duty and wanted to make sure you were okay."

"Thanks, officer. Yes, after you left I didn't see or hear anything out of the ordinary."

"Good, I wanted to see you before you saw this," he said as he handed her the newspaper that was laying on her front porch.

Ellen glanced at the front page. There was an article about a burglary in her neighborhood last night. One of her neighbors on the street behind her was locked in a closet while a man ransacked his home. "Oh dear, do you think the person who showed up here last night is the same person?"

"I don't know, ma'am but it's a strong possibility. I will be patrolling your area tonight, and hopefully, whoever is doing this will be caught."

"I'm so glad I had a security system installed last month. Thank you for coming by. I appreciate it."

After he left, Ellen made herself a cup of strong coffee. She needed it after having spent most of the night tossing and turning. She wished she would have taken Katelyn's advice on getting a dog. She could use the companionship and thought it would scare off any possible intruder.

Chapter 2

Donovan spent most of the night wondering who Jacques was. He didn't recall meeting him when he was in the café and Brigitte didn't mention hiring a new employee. She told him on several occasions that she had to keep the number of employees to a minimum to keep the menu prices where they were.

She was always afraid of losing customers to the new café a block away. Besides, the guy sounded as if Donovan woke him up. He was going to have to get some answers from her on their call tonight.

***

"Jacques! Why did you answer my cell phone last night?"

Jacques smiled and whispered, "But I am a lonely pastry chef, as you say."

"You made him have some suspicion. No more answering my phone!" she instructed rather firmly.

"Okay, I guess 'off with my head' if I do."

That made Brigitte smile and she brushed his shoulder as she walked away.

***

Katelyn filled Abby in on Amber's apologetic email and Ellen's stalker. They decided to check to see if Ellen was okay, and what the police found. Ellen was sitting in her living room getting ready for her physical therapist to arrive when they called. She quickly explained what happened to her neighbor and was glad the officer would be patrolling her neighborhood again this evening.

"I wish you would have gotten a dog since you live alone," Katelyn remarked.

"Well, I did have a security system installed last month, so if someone tries to get in, the alarm will go off and the police will be notified."

"That's a relief," Abby added.

Just then, the doorbell rang and Ellen knew she had to get off the phone. She didn't want the girls to know about her accident. She had fallen down the basement stairs a few weeks ago. She wasn't sure how something slippery got spilled on the top step but she took quite a tumble to the bottom of the steps. The bottom half of her body was greatly bruised, and her legs still ached and were unsteady.

"Katelyn and Abby, a friend is at the door. I'll let you know if I hear anything else, and hopefully, I'll see you both in six weeks."

"Okay Ellen, take care of yourself, and talk to you soon."

After they hung up, Abby looked at Katelyn and asked, "What do you think she meant by saying, 'Hopefully, I'll see you in six weeks?'"

"I wondered the same thing. I'm sure she didn't mean it the way we're taking it. She knows we registered for the cruise, and I'm sure she wasn't thinking about the stalker doing anything to her. I'll email her later today."

***

"Well, Amy, how do you think it's going? Will I be up walking around without this cane anytime soon?" Amy was Ellen's physical therapist and she knew Ellen would be disappointed in her report but she had to tell her something.

"I think you're coming along quite well. You did have a bad fall, and unfortunately, sometimes it takes a little longer for the body to heal."

"How much longer do you think?"

"Well, let me review my report with your doctor. But in the meantime, continue to use your cane, and I'll be coming back to check on you. It's very important to follow your exercise schedule as that will help in your recovery."

"In other words, it doesn't look like I'll be getting better anytime soon," Ellen said with sadness in her voice.

"We'll see, but let's not jump to conclusions. You've made a lot of progress these past two weeks."

As Amy got up to leave, Ellen was ready to show her out but Amy insisted she sit and rest. "Bye Ellen," she said as she walked out the door.

Amy quickly made a call on her way to her next appointment. No one answered so she left a message on the answering machine with a report on Ellen's progress. She made it a point to always call in after an appointment. This time she wasn't pleased with reporting her prognosis.

***

Amber woke up late and had to hurry to get over to Weldon's. He hated it whenever she didn't arrive on time. Sometimes she felt as though he was her boss instead of her writing colleague. When she knocked on the door,

23

Weldon didn't answer. Gee, I hope he's not too upset with me, she thought. She knocked again and still no answer. He had a beautifully landscaped yard and she walked around to the back patio.

There was a plate with a half-eaten bagel and a partial cup of coffee on the table but no sign of him. He always had a carafe of freshly brewed coffee ready for them, and sure enough, there was a bagel and a container of her favorite cream cheese for her. She thought perhaps he ran inside and would be out soon, so she sat down to start enjoying her breakfast. He was a grumpy old man but he did have a soft side. She finished eating, and still, no sign of him. She decided to knock on the back door in case he didn't notice she was there. No answer. She left her cell phone in her car and walked over to get it so she could call him. When he didn't answer his house phone, she dialed his cell number. It also went to voicemail but this time she left a message.

She decided to leave since she didn't know how long he would be gone. They didn't live that far from each other and she could always come back. She quickly gathered up her things as it looked like it might start raining any minute and ran to her car. She would try to call him when she got home.

***

Katelyn and Abby took off for the Bedford Falls mall at exactly five o'clock. They were planning on dining at the food court before trying on clothes. Abby talked nonstop about her assignment which so happened to be at the construction site of the new community being built. It seemed that appliances and materials were being removed. No one saw who was taking the items and the construction company was losing money to replace everything, as well as new homeowners who were finding other houses to purchase.

Katelyn filled Abby in on her afternoon call with Ellen. She thought it was best to call her directly instead of emailing her under the circumstances. Ellen said she was resting and was feeling better knowing the police would be staking out her neighborhood in unmarked cars. She assured Katelyn she would call her if anything out of the ordinary happened tonight.

***

"That looks beautiful on you, Katelyn!"

It was a low-cut sleeveless dress that was pretty but not her style. Abby, on the other hand, had an armload of dresses to try on. She handed her another dress that was more to Katelyn's liking. "Now this, I like," Katelyn said with a grin.

"Of course, you would, and I bet I can find a granny dress you'll love in the old lady's section!"

"Abby, that's enough! You never know who's beside us," she whispered.

Just then two older women entered the dressing room, but luckily, they didn't hear them. They both burst out laughing and decided on a couple of outfits. They were planning to go to a specialty swimsuit shop over the weekend.

***

Amber tried to reach Weldon again, but still no answer. She was worried and decided to go back over to his place to check on him. When she arrived, police cars were parked along the street and neighbors were standing outside.

25

"There she is!" someone called out.

"Yeah, she's the one who did it!" another person yelled.

Immediately, everyone turned their attention to Amber. She wondered why they were staring at her, and the next thing she knew, she was being pulled aside by two officers as the coroner's team carried out a body bag. Amber shrieked in horror when she saw it and knew it contained the body of her dear friend.

"Ma'am, please state your name."

"I'm Amber Jenkins," she managed to stammer out.

"We understand you were here earlier today; what can you tell us about your involvement with Weldon Hopper?"

She fell to the ground. She couldn't believe her eyes. "What happened to him?" The two officers each took one of her arms and got her to her feet. "Please tell me what is going on here? Why are you questioning me?"

The two officers exchanged glances and knew this wasn't going to be easy. "Ma'am, just answer our questions, please."

Shaking, she was able to blurt out, "I was here because Weldon and I were collaborating on a book together." She accepted a tissue from one of the officers and continued, "I was late getting here, and he didn't answer the front door." She paused to catch her breath. "I walked around to the patio and saw he had started eating his breakfast but he was nowhere in sight. He had a bagel set aside for me and some coffee." She started crying again and said, "Thinking he would be out any minute, I started to eat my breakfast." She took a deep breath and continued, "When I finished eating, he was still inside, so I tried reaching him again on my phone when he didn't answer the door. After that, I left."

"Interesting story. Why did you run off when you left?"

"I didn't run off! I noticed it was getting ready to rain so I may have hurried to my car. Why are you questioning me as if I'm a murderer?"

"It's our job to ask the questions, ma'am. We're letting you go for now but don't leave town."

"This is outrageous! Why aren't you out looking for the real murderer?" She tried to calm down before asking, "What happened to Weldon?"

"Ma'am, you'll find out all in due time; please don't make this any harder than it is."

As Amber was leaving, she noticed they were taking things out of Weldon's house. What happened to him? And why did the neighbors accuse her of any wrongdoing? She was clueless as to what was going on.

The next morning, two officers appeared at her door. They asked if they could come in. After informing her of Weldon's murder, they asked her about her relationship with him. Amber broke down and cried out, "Who would want to kill Weldon?"

After a brief talk, another officer showed up with a search warrant. They wanted to investigate her house looking for any clues that would lead them to believe she was involved. "This is getting absurd! I have nothing to hide! I just want you to find out who did this to my friend!"

She went into the kitchen and was sitting down at the table when an officer asked her for her computer password. She shakingly wrote it down and went back to reading the news on her cell phone to see if there was any information on what had happened. An email popped up from William telling her to hang in there with Weldon that he had his moments but jokingly told her not to kill him. A few minutes later, the original two officers entered the kitchen asking her to stand and handcuffed her while reading her rights. They saw the email and assumed she had something to do with Weldon's death. As they were taking her down to the police station, they asked her if she had any next of kin or someone she would like to call. All she could think of was Weldon and started crying.

After getting down to the police station, Amber made her statement, was fingerprinted, and given an unattractive uniform in exchange for her clothes. She was put into a cell with a woman who had gotten carried away at a nightclub the night before and swung a broken glass bottle at a bouncer. Luckily, she didn't harm him but she was angry at how she was being treated. Go figure, Amber thought.

She decided to call William since he sent the email that the officers read along with hers. She thought if anyone could be a character witness and explain the relationship between her and Weldon, he would certainly do. She was sure all of the authors in their group would be more than willing to help her if needed.

"Hello William, this is Amber."

"Hello Amber, how are you? Are you still planning on..."

She cut him off before he could go any further. "William, Weldon has been murdered. The police aren't telling me anything but I'm in jail. I need your help; I don't have anyone else to turn to."

Amber started sobbing and William jotted down all of the information so he could take the next flight. "Don't worry, Amber, I'll be there as soon as I can. I'm in London now, darling, but I'll see you soon. Don't say anything to anyone until I get there."

"Okay," she replied through sobs, "thank you, William."

After he got off the phone, he emailed Ellen, Donovan, and Katelyn. He was still in shock when they got on the zoom call an hour later. He explained he didn't have any of the details regarding why Amber was arrested for Weldon's murder. They all felt bad for their friend, and Katelyn volunteered to pick him up at the airport and take him to see Amber. His flight was getting in the next day at one o'clock at the Manchester Airport in New Hampshire. Katelyn would have an hour and a half drive to pick him up and decided to make hotel reservations where he was staying. She figured he would need all of the help he could get in clearing Amber's name.

That evening, Katelyn told Abby she was going out of town for a few days and taking Biscuit with her. After Abby heard what happened, she called her boss at the news station to see if there was any interest in a story. He jumped right on it and told her and her cameraman to go and be ready to report. He was hoping his station would be able to get more facts and be able to out-broadcast the other stations. Abby informed Katelyn of her assignment, and Katelyn decided to see if Biscuit could stay at Puppy Trails.

She knew with Abby along there was bound to be drama.

Chapter 3

The next day, Katelyn and Abby along with Jim, her cameraman, headed out for the Manchester Airport. Since it was a business trip, Abby got a news van. The whole way there, Abby and Jim discussed what was going on at the news station. It was a relief for Katelyn to be able to sit back and collect her thoughts on what was happening to Amber.

She felt sick to her stomach at the thought of Weldon being murdered, but she knew Amber wasn't the killer. It was going to be up to William and her to figure out who had done it.

***

Ellen kept in touch with Weldon over the years, especially after last year's murder mystery weekend. She noticed a recent change in him but he never told her if anything was bothering him. He didn't share much about himself, and she was glad he was working with Amber. Deep down, Weldon knew she missed her father, and he wanted to give her some guidance on her writing in his absence.

After another restless night of worrying about her friends and the neighborhood stalker, Ellen got up and quickly dressed to go downstairs to get the newspaper. She was eager to see if anything was reported. As soon as she opened the door, she saw Officer Bradford walking towards her house. He waved and gave her a thumbs up. She smiled knowing that meant no robberies occurred last night. That gave her a little peace of mind.

She went inside and decided to make some oatmeal to go along with her coffee. She was getting ready to eat when her phone rang. She heard a familiar voice say, "Hello Ellen, I hope I didn't wake you." It was Donovan. He was worried about Amber and was upset about Weldon's murder. "I feel like I need to be there for her," he stammered.

"I know what you mean; I feel the same way."

"Would you like me to fly in and then we can go to New Hampshire together?"

Ellen thought for a few seconds before answering. "Donovan, you know you're my dear friend," she started.

"Of course, I do."

"Well, I fell a couple of weeks ago and have been receiving physical therapy. I'm using a cane to get around now."

"Why didn't you say something? Are you okay to travel?"

"Well, I'm not sure. Please keep this to yourself as I'm not even sure I'll be able to go on the cruise."

"I'm going to find a flight and fly in as soon as I can. I'll text you my flight info and will be at your place in a jiffy. Don't worry about a thing, Ellen."

"Thanks, Donovan, I'll see you soon."

After they hung up, Ellen was glad Donovan was coming. He was always like a son to her. She was wondering about his French girlfriend and how she would feel about him visiting her but as far as she knew, she was in France. She finished her breakfast and was glad she called the cleaning service last week to come by today.

***

It was finally time for William's flight to arrive. Jim stayed inside the van and Katelyn and Abby waited inside the terminal by baggage claim. They were excited since it had been almost a year since they last saw him. Finally, they caught a glimpse of him behind some small children. They were talking and running around him, while he made funny faces making them laugh. He was such a nice guy, Katelyn thought. He saw them and put his hand up into the air. He walked over and hugged them both and it brought tears to Katelyn's eyes knowing that he wasn't there for a good reason.

He realized what she was thinking and kissed her forehead and said, "I know how you feel. We're going to get to the bottom of this."

After retrieving his luggage, they walked to the van. William was surprised to see a news van and Abby explained she was on assignment with her cameraman, Jim. William didn't know what to make of a news story about Amber's false arrest and Weldon's murderer on the loose. He decided to stay away from any cameras and was definitely not doing any interviews. Abby was Katelyn's sister but he had to draw the line, friend or not.

Katelyn sensed William's concern over Abby's news assignment and they were quiet during the short trip to the Hampshire Inn where they had reservations. Abby and Jim were staying at another hotel a few blocks away. After dropping them off, Abby told Katelyn she would call her after she was checked in. William was planning on taking an Uber to the prison as soon as they dropped off their luggage.

"William, I would like to go see Amber with you, if that's okay."

He was glad Katelyn wanted to go along. "Yes, I think Amber needs all of the support she can get right now. I'll call for a driver and we can head over in half an hour."

"Sounds good, I'll be ready."

Abby was anxious to get started on the story but sensed William wasn't so thrilled about her and Jim being there. After they dropped their bags off at the hotel, they took off for the police station to start doing some of their own digging.

**

Donovan's flight was supposed to take off at eleven o'clock in the morning. He was disappointed after he rushed to the airport to discover there was a flight change. Now it was rescheduled for one o'clock in the afternoon. He decided to take a walk around the airport as he thought about Brigitte. She seemed normal last night when he spoke to her. It was probably just as she said; Jacques was a tired pastry chef wanting to get some rest.

As luck would have it, he saw an old friend from his college days. They were on the same flight so they grabbed a burger and a beer from the pub near their gate. His buddy took his mind off of the recent current events running through his mind, and it was nice to catch up and recall the good times they had.

**

"I still don't know why I'm in here," Amber lamented to anyone who would listen.

"Seems to me they have something on you, sweetheart," her cellmate answered with a snicker.

"Please, do not call me that!"

33

"Oh honey, lighten up. There are worse places you could be. I was in the slammer in Georgia. You talk about a bad..."

"Please stop! I don't care to hear about you and your earthshaking experiences in or out of jail."

"Sure doll face, whatever you say," she said with a salute.

Amber picked up a book that was on the delivery cart that came by earlier. She couldn't believe they had one of her father's mysteries here in prison for the inmates to read. She read the dedication. 'To my daughter, Amber, may you always find success in everything you do. You have brought so much joy in my life, and I'm proud to be your father. Love, Dad.'

Amber started to tear up and her cellmate walked over and put her arms around her. Amber closed her eyes and cried uncontrollably on her shoulder. She wondered what her father would think of her now if he could see her.

***

William and Katelyn got into the Uber and were on their way to see Amber. Once they arrived, they went through security, signed in, and were given visitor badges. They were happy the process didn't take long. It was a small facility located on the edge of town.

Amber was informed she had visitors and breathed a sigh of relief. She couldn't imagine who the other visitor was and hoped it was someone who could be of help. As she walked down the corridor, all she could think about was the awful murder of her friend and being accused as his killer. When she walked into the room and looked across the glass wall, she saw William and Katelyn. She put her trembling hands to her mouth and started crying. They wished they could have comforted her but they were only able to speak to her using the mounted telephone on the wall.

Katelyn and William held the phone between them as they both wanted to hear what happened and assure Amber they were there for her. After calming down, she relayed the details of the morning she was at Weldon's for their writing session and how she couldn't find him. They found it interesting that she was eating the breakfast he laid out for her on the patio table, and apparently, he ate before she arrived. William, being the investigative type, asked her if she noticed anyone around since the neighbors said they saw her there. She thought back and couldn't recall seeing anyone outside. Amber mentioned that Weldon's backyard had a high fence, and Katelyn wondered how they saw her if she didn't see any of them unless they were looking over at Weldon's backyard through an upstairs window. It appeared the neighbors may have more information than they were sharing. Did they see Weldon having breakfast? Was he approached by anyone? Did they see him go inside his house? These were all things they needed answers to. Amber was glad she called William. He, along with Katelyn, had a lot of good questions and she was sure that they were going to find out the answers.

"Did you get an attorney yet?" Katelyn asked.

"No, I don't even know who to call. I've heard of an attorney by the name of Alan Bakersfield."

"Let us handle contacting him for you," William suggested. The guard informed them that their time was up, and Amber thanked them for coming. "We'll be back tomorrow, and hopefully, with news of an attorney," William said with a raised hand.

"Thank you both for coming!"

"Hang in there, Amber. We'll see you soon," Katelyn said as she waved goodbye. She and Amber both had tears in their eyes and William wished he could comfort them both at that very moment.

They decided to get a rental car to avoid relying on Ubers. After speaking with Amber, they knew they were going to need to stay in town longer than they had expected.

***

The cleaning service sent over two new employees.

"What happened to the other Maria?" Ellen asked.

"Oh, she's off today," the one who was wearing a name tag with Maria on it.

"I see your name is Maria too," Ellen added.

"No, ma'am, my name is Carmen but since I'm new, I didn't get a name tag yet."

"Oh, I see, and is your name really Stacy?" she asked the other.

"Yes, ma'am, it is. I guess we should get started now, Carmen," Stacy said, as she picked up a vacuum cleaner.

"Yes, of course, I won't keep you," Ellen remarked as she hobbled away.

***

Donovan enjoyed the time he spent with his friend, Rob, so the delayed flight turned out to be not so bad. He was able to switch seats before they boarded so they would be able to continue their conversation. They had a six-hour flight, and hopefully, it wouldn't be a long wait for a rental car. He didn't want to keep Ellen up too late waiting for his arrival.

He landed at the Kansas City Airport and was able to secure a car and was on his way to Ellen's house. It was around eight o'clock and he was starving. He saw a mom-and-pop restaurant that advertised homemade pizza and other Italian dishes, and decided to stop there since he was sure that Ellen had already eaten. He thought he'd call her once he placed his order.

"Hello, Ellen! I just got in and I'm grabbing a bite to eat before heading over to your house. I'm at a place called Mario's and was wondering if you had dinner."

"Yes, I ate hours ago. I highly recommend their pizzas and pasta dishes. I never had a bad meal there."

"Okay, good, I'll get on the road as soon as I finish my dinner."

After he hung up, he tried to reach Brigitte. She didn't answer so he left her another voice message.

"Here you go, sir. Do you need another drink?" The server was nice and Donovan was glad he found this place, especially since Ellen was fond of it. "Yes, I'll have another soda, please."

She hurried off to get him a refill while he began enjoying his pizza. He was definitely going to be taking some slices along for him and Ellen since their pizzas were huge. After he was finished, he pulled up the directions on his cell phone navigation app, and he was pleased to see he only had a thirty-minute drive. As he was traveling, he noticed there was hardly any traffic and he was able to make it to Ellen's place within twenty minutes.

He was about to call Ellen to let her know he was almost to her house when he saw someone running down the street in the direction he was heading. A couple of minutes later, he answered Brigitte's call when he saw Ellen was calling him.

He put her on hold to answer Ellen. "Hello Ellen, I'm almost to your house."

"Thank goodness! Hurry!"

"Why, anything wrong?"

"I think someone is looking in at me from the kitchen window."

"I'll be there in a minute. Stay put and stay away from the windows."

He got back on the call with Brigitte and told her he had an emergency to deal with and would call her back shortly.

Donovan turned his lights off and parked down the street from Ellen's place. He didn't want to scare off any intruder and was hoping it was just a harmless kid pulling pranks on the neighbors. He quietly closed the car door and grabbed the only weapon he could find; a tire jack that was on the floor behind the passenger seat. Normally, he would have thought the rental company did a lousy job cleaning out the car but he was glad it was left there. He walked down the street to Ellen's and noticed a figure standing beside the house looking in the window. He didn't want to be noticed so he went through the neighbor's yard.

Just then, a spotlight came on and a man carrying a gun emerged from the front door. "What do you think you're doing?"

Donovan was stunned to see someone and was afraid whoever was over at Ellen's house was getting inside. He immediately put his hands up with the tire jack falling to the ground. All of a sudden, he heard the police sirens.

"Sir, I mean you no harm! I was on my way to Ellen Stratford's house."

By this time, two police officers arrived and walked over to Donovan. "Put your hands behind your back!"

"Officers, I did nothing wrong," Donovan protested.

"He was carrying this," Ellen's neighbor said pointing down to the tire jack.

"You don't understand, I'm Ellen's friend and was on my way to her house."

"So, you were taking a shortcut through the neighbor's yard, I take it?"

Ellen was hiding inside her walk-in pantry. She wondered what was keeping Donovan but did as he suggested by staying away from any windows. She was thinking about opening the pantry door to see if she saw anyone when she heard the kitchen door opening. Why isn't the security alarm going off, she thought. She just had it checked when the company sent a technician out last week and everything seemed to be in order. She was scared and stayed still.

Whoever it was walked into the living room, and then she heard footsteps going upstairs. She hoped Donovan would get there soon. She didn't know what to expect if he didn't.

"Officers, let's walk over to Ellen's house and she can clear this up," Donovan suggested. "She thought someone was looking in her kitchen window when she called me. I'm afraid she may be in danger."

The officers agreed after checking his identification and the neighbor, whose name was Ben, followed behind. Once they arrived, they circled the outside and the officers radioed each other that they didn't see anyone. Donovan figured the person took off when the police arrived. They hoped whoever it was, wasn't hiding inside Ellen's home. The one officer knocked loudly on the kitchen door identifying himself. Ellen was relieved and scared at the same time. She was too frightened to leave the pantry and wished she had her cell phone with her. She wondered what the intruder was up to on her second floor.

After a few more knocks, the officers entered and began their search. They didn't know if there was someone armed in the house and they had their guns in position as they began their search. The one officer opened the pantry door and found a shaking Ellen holding a cane with her left hand to steady herself. She put her index finger to her lips and pointed upstairs. Donovan and her neighbor stayed in the pantry wanting to stay out of sight and hold onto Ellen, who was scared and very weak.

The officers made their way up the stairs trying their best not to make any noise. The third step from the top creaked, and all of a sudden they caught a glimpse of a person going out of the bathroom window. They yelled, "Stop right there," but the person made it out and jumped onto the nearby oak tree. The officers yelled down to Donovan and Ben that the person jumped out of the window, and by the time they looked outside, they saw a dark van swiftly pull up across the street for the person to get inside.

Unfortunately, no one got a good look at the intruder. The individual was wearing a completely black outfit with a matching hoodie jacket. The person appeared to be of small stature, so it could have been a female or a small male. The takeoff van was so fast, they only saw the color in the darkness.

Once everyone got inside, Ellen gave her statement. She explained that she noticed someone looking in the living room window the other night for the first time when the burglary occurred on a nearby street. Ellen and the officers did a quick search and found some jewelry and cash were missing from her safe. She was sad that they took the necklace given to her by her mother, who said it was passed down from her grandmother. The officers felt bad delaying their search by questioning Donovan, but he said he understood given the recent criminal activity in the neighborhood. Ben shook hands with Donovan and gave him his business card. He owned the local bakeshop and invited him and Ellen to stop by any morning for breakfast, on him.

The officers left and Ben walked Donovan down to his car. He was still carrying the tire jack just in case. He decided to take Ben up on his breakfast offer the next morning so they could check in on any more strange occurrences and to come up with a plan in case the intruder decided to pay another visit.

It was another restless night for Ellen. She hated thinking about someone coming inside her house and touching her things. The stolen jewelry couldn't be replaced. Soon, she dozed off. With Donovan in the house, she felt safe. She was exhausted and finally, the lack of sleep had overtaken her.

Donovan checked all of the windows and doors even though the officers already did. He was planning on walking around the outside of the house early the next morning to see if the intruder left any clues behind that the police missed in the darkness.

***

The next day, Abby dialed Katelyn's cell number. That's funny, she's not answering. She called the Hampshire Inn and was connected to her room. The phone rang and rang with no answer. Maybe she went out to lunch with William. She called Jim who was unpacking and asked him if he would like her to order room service so they could start to go over their game plan. She knew her boss would be checking in soon and wanted to be ready for his line of questioning.

After he spoke to Abby, Jim called his girlfriend, Jen to let her know how things were going. She laughed when he told her about the road trip with Abby. It was a joke between them knowing how over the top she can be, but Jim enjoyed her energy and was glad he got to work with her.

Abby talked the whole way through the lunch she had ordered. In between pauses, Jim asked her if she thought the local police would talk to her. She said she had an angle. She was hoping to mention to them that she knew Amber and could appeal to the viewers to come forward with any information they may have or seen on the morning of Weldon's murder. They finished eating and were ready to head down to the police station.

On the way, they passed the prison, which was in a separate building from the precinct. Abby was tempted to stop and see if Katelyn and William were there visiting Amber. She decided to stick to their plan and go directly to the precinct. She promised her boss she would try to get an interview and had to stay on track.

Once inside the station, the police officer behind the counter asked how he could help them. Abby explained the reason for their visit, and he made a call. In a few minutes, Sergeant Reynolds came out and they followed him back to his office.

"How can I help you?" he asked. Abby gave him her business card and filled him in on her relationship with Amber and Weldon. "Ma'am, I understand you want to help. It's very commendable you came all this way but I'm sorry to have to tell you that you wasted..."

"Sergeant Reynolds," she said, stopping him before he could go any further, "I assure you that if you want to keep an innocent woman locked up for a crime she didn't commit, Jim and I will leave right now. However, if you want

42

to try to bring the real murderer to justice, we will stay and do our best to help your department find the individual responsible for this tragedy!"

The sergeant looked up from his paperwork surprised at Abby's response. This gal has some spunk, he thought. The department is lacking manpower, and maybe with her having known the victim and the accused, she could help them with the investigation.

"Okay," the sergeant said, raising his right hand. "You can go out to Mr. Hopper's home with an officer and do a news story. Nothing is to be touched; you can stand in the backyard where it was reported they planned to meet. Do I make myself clear?"

"Yes sir," Abby flashed a smile of success. "When can we get started?"

Jim chuckled to himself. He loved watching her work. "I'll bring in Detective Miller who will be joining you."

After the sergeant left, Abby looked over at Jim. "Well, we did it, partner!" she exclaimed.

"No, it was all you! You truly are amazing to watch, my friend."

The sergeant returned a few minutes later and advised them that Detective Miller was off today. He sent him a text message and told Abby he would let her know when he heard back from him. He felt certain the detective would make himself available to them.

***

Once inside the van, Abby turned and gave Jim a high five. "Let's go take a quick drive around Weldon's neighborhood so we can see where it all happened. It doesn't hurt to get an early start investigating our story."

Jim laughed. He knew he was working with a real firecracker.

Chapter 4

The next morning, Donovan got up around six forty-five. He wanted to get an early start looking around Ellen's yard before she got up. He put on a light jacket, and headed out, walking around the perimeter of the house first. He was looking at the two footprints that were in the flower bed by the kitchen window. He took a photo of it on his cell phone when he was grabbed from behind. He turned around and saw a police officer.

This was getting old, he thought.

"What do you think you're doing?" the officer asked.

"Well, I'm trying to see if the intruder left any evidence behind last night."

By this time, the neighbor across the street was walking down their driveway. "Is that the burglar, Officer Bradford?"

Oh, gee, these people just love to jump to conclusions, Donovan thought.

"No, he's not," Ellen said as she opened her front door.

"Officer Bradford, this is Donovan, my friend who flew in late last night. The poor dear has been accused of being an intruder ever since he got here," she said loud enough for anyone outside to hear. The neighbor felt embarrassed and walked inside his house.

Ellen invited the officer to come inside for a cup of coffee so they could update him on the previous night's occurrence.

After they gave him a brief rundown, Officer Bradford apologized again to Donovan and said he was off duty last night and would keep a lookout for any strange occurrences tonight. He was hoping the intruder would be arrested soon so the community could finally get back to normal.

Donovan walked outside and was surprised to see the set of footprints were no longer there. He wondered how they disappeared. The only explanation had to be when they were inside filling Officer Bradford in on the previous night's activity, someone covered them up. He looked around and didn't find any other evidence. He walked inside and told Ellen that Ben invited them to breakfast and he was anxious to talk to him.

When they walked into the bakery, Ben was behind the counter ringing up a to-go order. After he finished, he waved to them to follow him to the back of the bakery. It was a parlor-type room that was beautifully decorated. He explained they used this area for teas and group events. After he brought in a plate of pastries and coffees, they got down to business.

"Did you see or hear anything else last night?" Donovan began.

"No, after the police left, all was quiet."

"Yeah, same over at Ellen's. I was outside by her kitchen window this morning and took this photo of a set of footprints before being grabbed by an Officer Bradford."

Ben let out a half-chuckle. "You've been having a rough time ever since you arrived in town. False accusations, false arrest, and being attacked!"

Donovan looked at Ellen and said, "The things you go through for friends!"

Ellen smiled and reached out her hand to touch his. Donovan continued and told him about the footprints disappearing after Officer Bradford left. "That's odd; you didn't see anyone before you went inside?"

"No, just a nosy neighbor across the street but he went inside when Ellen told everyone within earshot that I was her friend," he said with a smile.

They sipped on their coffee and enjoyed their pastries. Finally, Donovan asked about Officer Bradford.

"When does this Officer Bradford work? He said he was off last night and he didn't know about the robbery at Ellen's."

"He told me he usually works the swing shift but lately has been doing more night shifts," Ben advised.

"He came by the first night that I saw someone outside my living room window and stopped by the next morning to check on me," Ellen mentioned.

"I'm surprised he didn't know about what happened at your house last night. I would imagine he would check in at the precinct before going out on duty," Donovan added.

Ben said he thought he seemed like a good guy and was always around checking in with the neighbors. "I agree, he's been checking in on me ever since these robberies and intruder sightings have started." Ellen thought he was doing a good job of keeping everyone as safe as possible.

"That's good," Donovan said. He wished he would have had more time to look around before he showed up but it wasn't Bradford's fault Ellen invited him inside. He was going to have to keep an eye out for any suspicious behavior.

After they left, Donovan began questioning Ellen. "Has anyone been coming to the house lately?"

"Yes, the physical therapist and the ladies who come by twice a month to clean for me."

"Anyone acting suspicious or doing anything out of the ordinary?"

"No, not really. I love my physical therapist. In fact, it's almost time for today's therapy session."

"Good, I'd like to meet her."

"Who said it's a 'she'?" Ellen asked with a grin.

"Just a hunch, my dear, just a hunch!" They both laughed while Donovan continued to look around. This time he stayed inside where the jewelry and money went missing. Ellen didn't have the safe combination written down anywhere and he wondered how the intruder figured out the combination in such a short amount of time.

The doorbell rang and Donovan ran downstairs and volunteered to open it for her. "Hello, is Ellen home?" the therapist asked.

"Yes, of course, please come in. My name's Donovan O'Hara, a longtime friend of Ellen's."

"Nice to meet you, Mr. O'Hara. My name's Amy and I am here to check on Ellen."

"Come on in, dear," Ellen called from the living room chair. She got up and walked over to her exercise equipment that was in a corner of the room.

"How are you feeling today?"

"Well, I think the right leg is improving some, but the left leg is taking longer."

"That's normal. You probably fell harder on that leg and are favoring it. Let's do a quick exam before we get started."

"While you two ladies are working out, I want to see where you got hurt, Ellen. Where did the accident occur?"

"On the top basement step; be careful something was spilled and that's what caused my fall."

"Okay, I'll check it out."

Donovan opened the basement door and was surprised that Ellen spilled what appeared to be oil on the top step. He was getting ready to clean it up so it wouldn't happen again when his cell phone rang. It was Brigitte. He closed the door and told her he would be staying with Ellen while she recuperates. She was sad to hear about her accident and break-in and hoped that it took his mind off of his conversation with Jacques the other night. Donovan decided not to mention his plan, hopefully with Ellen, to visit Amber in New Hampshire.

Amy thought Ellen did make some progress when she examined her legs. She felt better knowing that Ellen had a friend staying with her and decided to show him the exercises she had printed so he could help her. "Anything to help speed up Ellen's recovery," he told her.

On her way out, he asked Amy if Ellen told her much about how she had fallen. "She wasn't sure how something got spilled on the step that caused the accident. She took quite a tumble, but I can see she is determined to get better."

He agreed and assured her he would work with Ellen on the exercises. After Amy left, Ellen was tired so Donovan was going to wait to ask her about the oil-type substance he discovered on the step. He decided to take a nap as well so he would be ready in case there were any more late-night visitors this evening.

***

Katelyn and William decided to go back to the scene of the crime - Weldon's. There was no one there, and Abby and Jim finished their look around the neighborhood about an hour ago. As they began walking up the cobbled path to the back patio, the next-door neighbor opened her window and through the screen, asked them what they were doing. William explained they were friends of Weldon's and were trying to find out what happened.

"I'll tell you what happened," she yelled through the window. "That woman writer he supposedly was working with poisoned him!"

Katelyn looked at William with a bewildered look. "And the police investigated and discovered this, I suppose," William added.

"Don't think those nitwits know what they're looking for but at least they had the common sense to lock her up."

"Thank you for the information. Have a good day." Katelyn was concerned all of the neighbors felt the same way about Amber and didn't want to continue their conversation.

After she closed the window, William said they better start their search for a top-notch attorney. "I agree, it seems the neighbors have it out for Amber from what we've heard so far."

William pulled up a search on his phone and found the attorney, Alan Bakersfield that Amber had spoken of. He had excellent reviews and from what was said on the internet, was only a few minutes' drive away. Instead of calling, they decided to drive over to the office and check it out.

The office was in an old Cape Cod-style house. It was restored beautifully and reminded Katelyn of her grandparents' home when she and Abby were children. Unfortunately, their home was destroyed in a fire shortly after their deaths. They walked inside and were greeted by an older woman whose nameplate read 'Sophia'.

"Hello, I'm William Blackwell and this is my friend, Katelyn Winters."

"Oh, I love your English accent," Sophia cooed.

"Thank you, ma'am. We are looking for an attorney for a friend," he continued.

As he was saying that a man in a suit walked out of an office. "Hello, I'm Alan Bakersfield. How can I help you?"

It was obvious he was listening in on their conversation and it appeared that he wasn't busy. He escorted them into the office he just emerged from. William began by telling him about Amber, who was locked up for the murder of Weldon Hopper.

"And how do you know Miss Jenkins?" he asked.

Katelyn filled him in on the murder mystery weekend, and how Amber and Weldon were recently collaborating on a book together. "Her father was a mystery writer as well, and he was friends with Weldon. After her father passed away, Weldon took her under his wing to help her, from what we understand."

"Hmmm, interesting. The word around town is she couldn't stand the man and was..."

"Weldon had an attitude and would belittle and upset people. Everyone who knew him felt he was difficult. But we all became close after things went badly last year at the Winchester Estate during our murder mystery weekend. After that, we all learned to accept Weldon for what he was."

"What was that if you don't mind my asking?"

Katelyn explained how they all learned to care about him after they were both kidnapped together and how he helped her to escape. "There are just some things that you can't explain. Like how he wanted to help me and showed me a lot of compassion during the kidnapping and then afterwards, he could revert back to his old self."

"I see, I want to help but it's going to take a lot of work."

William shook his head in agreement and told him they understood and would do whatever they could to help.

"What are you doing for lunch today? I have a full schedule but I can have Sophia order food from the deli down the street and we can continue our conversation."

"Sounds like a plan; the sooner we get started, the better off for Amber," William responded.

"Great, I'll have Sophia bring in the menu and we'll get started."

Katelyn and William started from the beginning of their meeting with Weldon and Amber last year and ended telling him about their recent trip to meet with Amber and the neighbor's comments from earlier.

"It's a tough crowd around here," Alan commented. "Everyone thinks they're a know-it-all and unfortunately for Miss Jenkins, she's an outsider. Did the neighbors give the police any concrete evidence that you're aware of?"

"There was an email that Amber sent out to everyone in our author group and in it, she stated that there are days she could just kill him. We think that is the evidence they found linking Amber to his murder."

"That's interesting; how many times do people say that they could just kill someone but never mean it?" The attorney was right; it was a normal thing to say when someone irritated you to no end. But they had to prove her innocence.

"Let me get the police report and any evidence they have. I can have a messenger pick it up this afternoon and meet with you tomorrow afternoon. I have another full schedule but I could see you in my office at, let's say, one o'clock."

William quickly thanked him, and they both shook his hand as they walked out of his office.

"Man, that was easier than I thought it would be," Katelyn remarked on their way to the car.

"Do you think it was too easy, my American friend?"

"I hope he's sincere and not like the others who want to keep Amber locked up."

"Me too, it might be my English background, but I hope he doesn't have a secret agenda."

"I think we should keep digging just in case your instincts are right."

"Agreed, Katelyn, let's go do some investigating on our own."

***

After napping, Donovan asked Ellen about the oily substance he found on the top step. "What do you think it is?"

"I have no idea. I never go down to the basement and was only going down when I heard a noise coming from there the night of my accident."

"What did it sound like?"

Ellen took her time before answering and said she thought it sounded like a window opening and heard something being moved across the floor. "What do you think it was?"

"I'm not sure as I only have an old chair and some other furniture that's been down there for years."

"Do you remember anyone going down there from your cleaning crew?"

"No, not that I know of. I only have them clean the first and second floors."

"Any utility workers or repairmen down there lately?"

"No, but I had a security system installed last month. I don't recall either of the two men going down there but I was having a physical therapy session on the day they began the installation. You don't think they had anything to do with it, do you, Donovan?"

"I don't know, but we can't leave anyone out. How did you find their company?"

"The one man was going around the neighborhood advertising their services. He said they were installing a system for one of my neighbors and was offering a considerable discount to anyone who signed up that day."

"Okay, I'm going to need his business card and the information on the cleaning service you use. I'll run a check on them to see if they're legit."

"Okay, I have the SOS Security System's business card and I have the number for the cleaning service. I've been using them for years and doubt there is any problem with them."

After Donovan received the information, he made a call to the cleaning service first. It appeared that the original Maria who worked on cleaning Ellen's home moved back to her hometown in Mexico. She didn't leave a forwarding address, however, she worked for the cleaning company for the past ten years with a glowing report from their customers. Next, he called the company that installed the security system in her house. He had to leave a voice message and was assured they would get back to him by the end of the day. Donovan was concerned the men could be involved and was anxious to hear back.

At seven o'clock, Donovan finally received a call from Dave, one of the technicians who installed the security system. Donovan asked him about the installation of the system and informed him that Ellen's home was broken into the previous evening. He apologized for the system error in not alerting her or the police of the intrusion. He promised to stop by the next morning to see what was wrong as he remembered everything was in working order when he tested it. Donovan wasn't sure if he believed him but thanked him before hanging up. He was going to be watching him just to make sure everything was functioning properly before he left.

Ellen was ready to go to bed at nine o'clock but she stayed up until ten since she had company. Donovan hadn't heard from Brigitte since the other night so he decided to call her.

"Bonjour ma Chère!"

Brigitte didn't seem like herself and he asked her what was wrong. She started crying and admitted that Jacques was her ex-boyfriend and they decided to try to work through their problems. He was taken by surprise as she always acted like Donovan was the love of her life. "Au revoir, Brigitte," he said as he hung up. It wasn't easy saying goodbye and letting go but he knew he had to walk away.

He was wide awake now.

The conversation with Brigitte made him antsy and he was glancing out the windows making sure no one was watching from the outside. He stayed up until two o'clock before he finally dozed off. He figured since the previous sightings occurred earlier in the evening, he was safe to go to bed. He was determined to find out who was doing this and to forget about Brigitte.

Chapter 5

At seven o'clock in the morning, Officer Bradford swung by to check on Ellen.

Donovan, who had been sleeping on the sofa in the living room answered. "Hello, how can I help you, officer?" Officer Bradford was surprised to see him answer the door and asked if Ellen was home. "Yes, she is, but she is sleeping; can I help you?"

"Uh no, I was wondering if she noticed anyone around her home last night."

"No, we didn't see anyone."

By this time, Ellen appeared in the living room and called out to him. "Good morning, Officer Bradford, how are you doing this fine morning?"

"Hello Ellen, I was just stopping by to check on you."

"Thank you, officer, as you can see my good friend, Donovan, is still here and plans to stay to see me through my recovery."

"That's wonderful," he replied as he extended his hand towards Donovan to shake his. "I'm glad Ellen will have someone staying with her, especially after her fall down the basement stairs. Take good care of her!" And with that, the officer said his goodbyes and left.

"That was so nice of him to stop by," Ellen remarked.

"Yes, it was," Donovan agreed, "I'm glad there's a police presence in your neighborhood."

"I hope they soon catch whoever is behind this; I can't wait for things to get back to normal around here," she added.

At nine o'clock, Dave showed up to check Ellen's security system. He thought it was odd that the alarm didn't go off when Ellen heard the noises coming from the basement. He tested it a few times in various locations outside of her home, and each time, the alarm sounded. Donovan thanked him for coming out and Dave asked them to call if it malfunctioned again.

After he left, Donovan went upstairs to his bedroom and began making a list of people who have been inside Ellen's home. It wasn't adding up and he was going to have to be more observant when anyone came over.

He joined Ellen downstairs and asked her if she'd like to go see Ben at the bakery for breakfast. It was getting late and they hadn't had their morning coffee yet. He needed it after being up most of the night. He definitely felt like a nap was in order for the afternoon.

"Morning," Ben called out to them as they entered the bakery.

"Good morning, neighbor," Ellen replied.

They placed their order of muffins and bottomless coffees before Ben was able to join them. "How goes it?" he asked.

"Well, nothing to report at Ellen's place last night."

"Did you see this morning's paper?" Ben asked.

"We didn't have a chance to look at it yet. We had a busy morning with Officer Bradford stopping by and the technician from the security company testing out my alarm system again."

"Wow, you two have been busy," Ben replied.

57

"Any break-ins reported?" Donovan was hoping the police would have a suspect by now to put Ellen and the rest of the neighbors at ease.

"Well, another robbery at the McClellan's house around three this morning."

Donovan looked at them afraid to ask, "Where do they live? I was up until two and didn't hear anything and figured it was safe to go to bed."

"They're about five doors down on the opposite side of the street from my house," Ellen answered.

"I think the police need to be patrolling the neighborhood more with these break-ins happening almost nightly." Donovan thought it was ridiculous that this had been happening and no one was in custody yet.

"It's almost like they know when the cops take their breaks," Ben commented.

"I think something is off, but I don't know what it is. What are the other neighbors saying?" Donovan asked.

"I think it's time we get the neighbors together to find out!" Ben suggested.

"Agreed, a neighborhood watch group would probably be a good idea since the police obviously need help," Donovan added. "I think we should hold a meeting with the neighbors today."

Ben agreed and added, "We shouldn't meet at anyone's house to raise suspicion."

"Yes, I agree. Ben, can we meet here?" Donovan asked.

"Sure, I close at six and we can meet in the basement where we have club meetings."

"Good, Ellen and I can get in touch with the neighbors, and hopefully, everyone can make it tonight."

"Do you think we should invite Officer Bradford or someone from the police force?" Ellen asked.

"I think we should start with just our neighbors, for now, Ellen. I think the police need to be watching our homes while we're all away," Ben replied.

"Good idea, you never know when the intruders will show up."

After they left, Ellen got her telephone book out that she had for ages. Since she didn't call her neighbors often, she didn't have their numbers saved in her cell phone. Everyone she contacted was concerned and interested in attending tonight's meeting and joining the watch group but since it was such short notice, some of them had other plans for the evening. They wanted to be updated on what was discussed and said they would reach out to Ellen the next day.

Donovan called Ben and informed him of the community's interest. Another neighbor owned the restaurant next door to Ben's and said they could supply a sandwich platter, and Ben was going to bring down the leftover pastries. They wanted the neighbors to have a bite to eat since the meeting may go a little long.

At six o'clock, the neighbors began coming into Ben's bakery. He had a back door that led to the basement so no one had to enter through the front door. He didn't want it to appear to others that he was still open for business. Once everyone gathered, the meeting began. The neighbors who had break-ins were the first to speak. There was a total of eight robberies in the past two weeks. Mr. Smith claimed that he lived in the neighborhood for the past twenty-five years and never had a problem. Mr. McClellan agreed that it was unheard of that anyone would commit so many robberies in their community.

"It's outrageous!" Mrs. Gates chimed in. "What are we going to do about it?" she asked.

"What do you think about the job the police are doing?" Mrs. Jones asked. "It seems like they show up after the crimes have been committed," she added.

"We think they're doing the best they can with the manpower they have," Ben replied. "That's why we're here trying to set up this watch group to help catch the robbers before anyone gets hurt. We've been lucky so far that only personal items and cash have been stolen. It's a scary situation and we have to put an end to it."

Donovan stood up and introduced himself. He explained he and Ellen spent the afternoon discussing what was reported. He further explained that since the police are not around during the actual break-ins, it was up to the community members to start a neighborhood watch group. He pulled out a map of the area that was blown up and he had all of the houses labeled with the families' names and which houses were to be included in each separate group.

"For example, if we have a dozen houses on each street, we should have two watch groups. We take turns watching for any out-of-the-ordinary occurrences, no matter how trivial they seem. We realize some of you have hectic schedules with jobs, children, and other responsibilities, so however much time you can give to protecting the community would be appreciated. We hope this sting operation won't take long."

As soon as the word 'sting' was used a group of men raised their hands to help. "I'm sure my husband is thinking he'll be a secret agent like in the spy movies he's fond of," Mrs. Smith whispered to Ellen. Regardless of their reasoning, Ellen was glad the men were wanting to help catch whoever was terrorizing their community.

Everyone enjoyed the food and the time slots on the watch sheets were completely filled out. Neighbors received a telephone listing of who to call in case of emergencies or if someone needed help filling their shift or during their shift. All in all, it was a productive meeting.

Tonight, the schedule was set-up for ten four-hour shifts. It was going to be a long night and Donovan volunteered to be available and check-in with all the teams from nine o'clock until one in the morning, and Tim, who lived on Maple Street, volunteered to take over beginning at one o'clock. They felt it was necessary to have someone checking in on all of the teams since the police weren't able to handle the investigation on their own.

Ellen and Donovan made a quick stop for coffee supplies and snacks on their way home. They wanted to have enough hot beverages on hand to fill a couple of thermoses and individual bags of snacks for the volunteers. They wanted to do all they could to bring an end to these break-ins that were happening in the neighborhood.

The first shift was uneventful. Donovan made his rounds and by doing so, he met a lot of the neighbors. Most of the volunteers were men, however, a lot of their wives stayed up with them. He even found a few of them had read some of his books and was thrilled when a couple of them had hard copies for him to sign.

When Tim took over, Donovan was tired. The nap he planned to take in the afternoon didn't materialize since he was busy getting ready for the six o'clock watch meeting. He hoped Tim didn't need his help as sleep was what he needed most. He reminded him to call his cell if he saw anything suspicious. Tim also knew Officer Bradford would be on duty so he could always reach out to him.

At around two o'clock, there was a sound coming from the Andersons. Tim looked and saw a pair of legs going through the basement window and immediately called Donovan. He didn't want to call the Andersons in case the intruder would hear their telephone ringing. After reaching

Donovan, Tim notified the police, and an officer was being dispatched. They said it would be less than ten minutes for them to get there. Donovan jumped into his clothes and made it over in five minutes, meeting Officer Bradford as he arrived. Tim showed them where the intruder entered the home, and Officer Bradford reached for his gun while knocking on the front door. Donovan wondered if he would scare the Andersons when they answered but Bradford was the officer and had experience in these types of situations.

While they waited at the front door, Donovan walked around to where the intruder had entered the home. He saw a figure throw a large backpack on the grass and then quickly got out of the window and ran towards the back fence. He yelled for Tim and Bradford but by the time they got there, it was too late. The Andersons opened the door and didn't realize anyone was in their home. After a quick inspection, they noticed some of their smaller antiques were missing. Everything taken had been in their bar area on the bottom level. They were glad no one was hurt, and Bradford began filling out his report. After they left, Donovan wished he would have taken the second shift, but he had confidence that Tim did all he could. Maybe they should have two people assisting the volunteers per shift, he thought. He wasn't sure why Dan, who was assigned to watch this section, didn't see anything.

After Bradford left, Donovan and Tim sat down at the kitchen table with the Andersons. Donovan didn't know their first names and found out they were Pat and Ed. Dan finally showed up and apologized for falling asleep. They knew Ben was up and at his bakery already. Ed dialed his number and told him about the robbery. They decided to meet at six o'clock at the bakery that evening. Something had to be done. Pat was a stay-at-home mom and said she would email all of the neighbors regarding the meeting. This time, Donovan was going to be prepared with an agenda.

When Donovan got back to Ellen's, he told her to wake him around noon. He knew it was going to be another long night and he wanted to be in tip-top shape.

Ellen thought he looked tired and decided to let him sleep until he woke up. At two o'clock, he finally got up. He was glad for the extra hours; he hadn't realized how exhausted he was. Ellen was preparing some sandwiches in the kitchen when he walked in.

"Good afternoon, sunshine," she greeted him. "Did you have a nice rest?"

"Yeah, thanks for letting me nap a little longer. I didn't realize how tired I was." He sat down at the table to look at the newspaper. He noticed she was moving around without her cane. "Hey, should you be doing that?" he said as he pointed to her cane in the corner of the room.

She laughed and said that during her physical therapy session this morning, Amy felt as though she was ready to hang it up for a few hours a day.

"That's great, Ellen! Just don't overdo it."

"Yes, yes, I learned my lesson and I'll certainly be watching where I step from now on."

She knew what Donovan was looking for and told him to turn to page two. The story read: *Another robbery has been reported in Homestead last evening. The police have been searching for the suspect who appears to be making a mockery of the police department.* The story continued stating that the officer who had been reporting the incidents has been just missing the break-ins but they feel certain they will find the suspect soon.

"It makes me wonder if it's an inside job," Ellen said as Donovan put the paper down. "But who?"

"Ellen, I've been thinking the same thing, too. We are having another neighborhood watch meeting tonight at the bakery. How about we contact the police to get an officer to attend? It seems like every robbery is called in and it takes a while for an officer to show up. With these break-ins occurring almost every other night, you would think they'd have more officers patrolling the neighborhood."

There was a moment of silence between them. "That's true. Who do you think should call them?" he asked, following up his original thought.

"How about Ben, he knows everyone in town with his bakery business."

"Okay, I'll let him know," Donovan assured her as he texted him.

Ben answered back almost immediately. Donovan asked if he could meet him before the meeting to go over a few things. The bakery slowed down at four so Ben told him he could come over any time after that. Donovan said he'd pick up some takeout from the Chinese restaurant for dinner and he and Ellen would be there at four-thirty. Ben was tasked with coming up with any agenda items for tonight's meeting, and Donovan and Ellen would be prepared with their items.

At four o'clock promptly, Donovan and Ellen left to go pick up their takeout order and then head over to the bakery. All afternoon, Donovan and Ellen worked on topics to be discussed at the meeting. They were anxious to see if Ben had any additional items. Once they arrived at the bakery, Donovan texted Ben so he would meet them at the basement door entrance.

Ben opened the door and helped Ellen into the room. She was back to using her cane and took a seat at the table while Donovan and Ben unpacked their entrees. Ben had his laptop ready to go with his agenda items listed. As they ate, Donovan began to read their items:

Break-ins have been occurring frequently with limited police presence; Length of time it takes for police to arrive when called; SOS Security system recently installed but not working when the break-in occurred at Ellen's; People coming and going into houses that have been robbed – any coincidences; Oil spilled on Ellen's basement step.

Ben thought the items Donovan read were the major concerns. He added:

Suspect sightings – male or female; Van – any descriptive information on the vehicle.

They continued to brainstorm until the others arrived. Ben ran upstairs to grab the leftovers that didn't sell that day, and Ed and Pat brought in some fresh lemonade.

"Thanks, everyone for coming again this evening," Ben began. "As you know, the Andersons' home was robbed last evening. Donovan, Ellen, and I have been working on an agenda to help us focus on what we know and don't know. We invited an officer from the police department, and it appears he hasn't made it yet, so we'll get started."

"If you're looking for Officer Bradford, he's off today and I think his shift usually starts around eleven," Tim commented.

"Okay, thanks, Tim."

They started down through the list. They were all concerned about the number of robberies occurring and their frequency. They also felt that the police presence was minimal considering all of the reports, and how slow their response time was. They appreciated Officer Bradford for his concern and for taking down their incident reports. Donovan sent a paper around to see who used the same security system company as Ellen. He also asked who was the original homeowner to use them as they went door-to-door advertising a special since they were already in the neighborhood doing work for one of their neighbors. Everyone looked at each other and said they were all given the same story.

"That's odd," and then Donovan asked, "Everyone who has had a break-in, did your system alarm go off?"

"Mine did, but it went off after the robbery," Barry advised.

"I didn't hear mine go off," Sylvia reported. "So, I called the company and a man came out and tested it. He thought it had a faulty part and replaced it. It worked after he fixed it."

Donovan smelled a rat. "Besides Dave, did he work alone or did he have a partner?"

Everyone answered there was another man who Dave said was his helper. "I'll take care of looking into this company," Ben volunteered.

"Great, let's move on," Donovan suggested.

Next on the list was the cleaning company that Ellen used. A few of them also used this service and only one other neighbor was robbed besides Ellen. No one had any medical personnel stopping by recently.

Ben asked if anyone had any information on the suspect or a description of the van or driver that the robber used. It was always pitch black that time of night, and the clothes he wore were dark in color. The van was black as well and no one could see anything to identify it.

Donovan asked if anyone had security cameras installed around their home. "Yes, and I gave the tape to the police for their investigation," Barry shared.

"Did you hear anything from them afterwards?" Ben asked.

"No, in fact, they doubted if they'd be able to see anything due to the time of the robbery and it was a foggy night."

"So, they didn't call you yet? How about you get the tape back from them and let us examine it," Donovan asked. "Sure thing, I'll stop by tonight on my way home."

"Great," and with that, Ben wrapped up the meeting asking everyone who signed up for tonight's watch to contact Donovan if they can't keep their shift or if they get tired. Dan felt bad as he knew he was referring to him falling asleep last night.

When Barry arrived at the police station, no one was on duty who could help him. He was irritated that they took his tape from the night of his break-in and acted like it was an inconvenience for them to fill out a report requesting his own personal property back. He wasn't happy, to say the least.

After he left, he called Ben. Ben thought he should ask Officer Bradford for it since he seemed to be the only one on the force who showed an interest in their community. Since Bradford was off that night, Barry was going to be on the lookout for him the following evening.

When Ellen and Donovan got home, they created a board of all of the possible suspects. It was similar to what they created when they were writing one of their mysteries. Underneath each name, they listed their involvement in the community and why they were considered a suspect.

The first name on the list was Dave and his helper from the SOS Security System. Reasons given were the systems malfunctioned during the break-ins or didn't work at all, and they lied about someone in the community originally hiring them. Second, the police department wasn't giving them the manpower needed to canvas the neighborhood regularly and their response time was slow when a robbery was reported. They probably didn't even review Barry's surveillance tape of the night of his burglary. The cleaning service Ellen used was a long shot as only one other neighbor that was robbed used that service. But they couldn't dismiss it yet.

Ellen wanted to stay awake as long as she could to keep Donovan company. She brewed a fresh pot of coffee and had some baked goods from Ben's bakery. She kept dozing off in her recliner but refused to go to bed. She wanted to help if she could.

At midnight, Donovan heard a strange noise outside. The only lights that were on was a night light in the hallway and another one at the top of the stairs. He didn't move. Ellen was in a deep sleep. The noise sounded like something was moving around on the side of the house where the basement window was. Then he heard a voice speaking low and unintelligible. Another voice answered and was a little louder. "Keep it down!" was what he heard. The other person didn't say anything in response.

Donovan quietly got up from the sofa and made his way over to the basement door. He remembered the oil spill was still on the top step and doubted if he could go downstairs quietly. He thought his only chance of catching whoever they were was trying to sneak out the kitchen door. He was going to have to disarm the security system and quickly make his way around to the side of the house. As soon as he put in the code, he opened the door trying not to alert the intruders or awaken Ellen. He closed the door as quickly as he could. He was carrying his cell phone and was ready to call the police when someone came up and hit him from behind.

It was the last thing he remembered before waking up in the ambulance.

Chapter 6

"How do you feel?" an EMT asked him.

"What happened?" Then Donovan's mind flashed back and he remembered being hit from behind. His head was aching. Ellen was being consoled by Pat and Ed Anderson, and Donovan called out to her. "Ellen, I'm okay."

She was so happy to hear his voice and rushed to his side. "What were you thinking going outside alone?"

"I guess I should have called for backup. They didn't happen to find the guys who did this, did they?"

By this time, Dan walked up and asked if he saw or heard anything before he was attacked. "No, I only heard them talking when I was inside."

"What did they say?" Ed asked.

By this time, Donovan's head was starting to throb. The EMTs told the men he needed to rest and closed the doors of the ambulance. The police were talking to the neighbors to find out any information they possibly had. They were going to head over to the hospital shortly afterwards to take down Donovan's statement.

Ben walked Ellen inside her home and asked if she needed anything. It was getting close to the time he normally got up to go to work. She said a shot of whiskey would do, and he looked at her as if she was serious. "No, Ben, I'm fine. You go home and get some rest. I know you have an early morning." He was getting ready to lock the door when the Andersons stopped by.

"We just wanted to check on Ellen before going home," Pat said. She put her hand on Ellen's shoulder and told her to call if she needed anything.

After they left, the rest of the neighbors walked to their houses. Except for two unnoticed individuals who were watching from a distance. They noticed Ellen was left at home alone. They walked to their van that was parked a few blocks away at a convenience store parking lot. They needed to get their plan in order as time was running out. They weren't happy about knocking out the guy that was staying with her but he was getting in the way and nothing could go wrong with their plan.

After they arrived back at their van, they saw a note underneath their windshield wiper blade on the driver's side. The driver grabbed the note and they both got inside. The note read: *'You idiots. Can't you do anything right? Get it done now while the coast is clear.'*

They knew what the note meant. With the guy they attacked being in the hospital and the police there probably taking down his statement, now would be a good time to finish the job. Besides, the money they were being paid was badly needed. They wanted to get out of this town pronto and put all of this behind them.

They knew they had to drive the van closer to Ellen's house. They parked on Maple Street. At the end of the road was a small overflow parking area. They didn't see anyone, and luckily, it was still pretty dark outside. They walked the short distance down the street, mindful of seeing anyone outside or peering through a window. Once they reached Ellen's, the plan was to go down inside the basement, grab what they were looking for, and get out. When they arrived, no lights were on, just the glow of what appeared to be nightlights that they noticed earlier. They walked around to the basement window, still not seeing anyone. They had already loosened the window earlier and were glad they could easily climb into it, grab what they needed, and get out. The job should be a piece of cake, they told their boss before they left the convenience store lot.

They easily got inside, making sure beforehand that the alarm was not activated for this window. They walked around the basement as quietly as they could. Their boss desperately needed a piece of paper and they were being paid to find it.

They searched through the piles of papers inside the old cardboard boxes and looked in the old furniture in case it was hidden in between a cushion or inside an old filing cabinet. They weren't happy it was taking so long. They heard a noise coming from outside. It was a newspaper boy riding his bike dropping off the morning's edition. They knew that if they stayed too much longer, their cover was going to be blown. They took one more look around the basement and knew they needed help. One of them decided to send a text message to their boss while the other continued the search. While waiting for an answer, the other guy began looking in an old tool chest. He thought maybe the evidence was hidden inside one of the drawers. They walked around the basement checking everywhere they could think of and came up with nothing. Finally, a reply was received from the text message. It read: *'Look underneath the fourth step from the top.'* They immediately began looking there trying to keep the noise level down. Lucky for them, Ellen was sleeping in her bedroom and it would have been very difficult for her to hear them. They found some tools they needed from the chest and began loosening the wooden step.

Ben was getting ready to take off for the bakery and noticed a light on in Ellen's basement. That's strange, he thought. I'm surprised it wasn't turned off when the police left. He didn't think anything more about it as he drove to work. He had a lot of special orders that were being picked up this morning and one of his bakers called in sick.

The step didn't have anything hidden in it. They decided to try the third step in case they made an error. This step didn't cooperate as easily as the other one and they had to work harder to remove the wood. It came up empty. This is ridiculous, they thought. They were going to try the fifth step when they heard Ellen's voice.

"Anyone down there?" she called from the kitchen.

They froze with the tools in their hands. When she didn't hear anything, she picked up the phone and dialed the police. She was put on hold and then was told they would dispatch an officer in the vicinity. They asked her to stay on the line since she was home alone.

After a few minutes, Officer Bradford arrived. He heard the report on his radio and came over immediately. "Good morning, Ellen. So, I understand you heard some suspicious noises in your basement. Do you mind if I take a look?"

"Certainly not, but be careful. I think whoever it was is still down there."

He said he would be careful not to step on the top step remembering the oil spill. Ellen thought back and recalled him saying that before, but she never remembered telling him about it. She must be getting forgetful in her old age, she thought.

He started down the stairs and noticed the two steps that were torn apart. He wasn't expecting to see this. He wondered what was going on down there before he arrived. The two men were still in the basement over by the furnace. They didn't think anyone would walk over towards them but they were prepared with a hammer and crowbar in case someone did. They didn't want to cause any more injuries unless they had to.

"It's the police. Anyone down here?" he called out when he reached the bottom. The men didn't move. Then he said, "I can make this easy for you. Come out and we'll talk about it."

Still no answer.

By this time, two other officers showed up. Ellen told them that Officer Bradford was already down in the basement where she heard the noises. Before she could advise them of the oily step, the first officer flew down the stairs, slipping on the top step and falling through the fourth step. The second officer tried to help by stepping on the first step and slid into the third step. Officer Bradford turned his attention to the two officers and the other two men were able to get out through the basement window. Lucky for them, they escaped unseen.

Officer Bradford asked Ellen to call and report 'officers down and need help' while he looked around outside for the intruders. He noticed they must have gotten away and went back inside to see how long until the paramedics and police would be there. At that time, they heard the ambulance coming down the street, and Ellen was relieved the officers, who were still stuck in her basement steps, would be rescued. Officer Bradford told her he was going to look around the neighborhood for the intruders and ask the neighbors if they saw anything. He assured her they were doing their best to solve the case.

When the paramedics arrived, they had to act fast so the officers didn't fall all the way through. They were hanging on in between the other steps.

Ellen went outside to see if Officer Bradford found anything but he must have gone further down the street.

She was certain he would stop by after he finished his search. She hoped one of her neighbors saw something that would help them catch whoever was tormenting their neighborhood.

The paramedics were able to safely pull the officers out of the steps. They were sore and were taken to the hospital. On their way out, they thanked Ellen and wished they could have caught whoever was inside her home. She said it was all due to Officer Bradford's quick thinking that they were safe. They gave each other a bewildered look as they were being loaded up into the ambulance.

After a quick look around, Officer Bradford made a quick stop at Ellen's. He informed her that whoever it was, they must have made a run for it, and he doubted with all of the police action at her home in the past several hours that they would be back. She thanked him again and asked if he was going to be on duty that night. He informed her that he would before taking off. She was surprised he was in an unmarked vehicle and not a police car. She figured he must be doing some undercover work for the department.

At nine o'clock, Donovan called from his hospital room. He was able to be released, and Ellen was anxious for him to get home. Shortly after his call, Officer Bradford stopped by one last time to check on her before going home to get some rest before his next shift. She told him the good news, and he offered to pick him up and bring him back to her place. She was relieved since she didn't want to call for a taxi or Uber, and she wasn't able to drive with her leg injuries.

"No problem, Ellen, glad to do it." As he took off, Ellen decided to make a welcome home breakfast for Donovan.

Before leaving for the hospital, Officer Bradford changed clothes and made a quick call. He wanted to get Donovan out of there before the two officers were admitted. He was sure they would be in the emergency room getting checked out before being treated as they looked to be in bad shape. He wanted to get in and out of there so he wouldn't spend a good part of his morning answering questions.

Donovan looked up and saw Officer Bradford and he explained he was there to pick him up as he was worried about Ellen's legs. He said his first name was Brian and he could call him that since they were practically friends. Donovan laughed and agreed they had been through a lot together. After Donovan signed the discharge papers, Brian helped him into his wheelchair and was able to get him down to his car before the police arrived to question him. Brian assured him that they would send an officer by Ellen's or he could take his statement once they arrived if he felt up to it.

Donovan was feeling much better. The pain medication for his head was finally working and he was given a prescription to fill. After getting into the car, Brian received a call. Donovan wasn't paying much attention as he was tired and wanted to take a nap. As Brian talked, he noticed Donovan laying his head down on the back seat of the car. His eyes were closed and Brian knew he could let the others know to move in that the coast was clear.

"Okay, we tried the third and fourth steps and there's nothing there. Now where should we look?" the one man asked.

"That's where it has to be. I don't care if you have to tear the whole place apart! Keep looking!" Brian said angrily.

He knew he had to keep Donovan asleep as once the meds wore off, he'd have to take him home. Donovan heard little bits and pieces of the conversation, but unfortunately, sleep was taking over. He wished he could have stayed awake but his body was exhausted.

At Ellen's, the two men had to sneak back in again, but this time, it was broad daylight. They were going to have to wear their SOS Security System outfits and tell Ellen they needed to check her alarm system once again. This was getting old and they hoped this was the last time they had to do it. Bradford had the easy job; being Mr. Nice Guy while they looked like the incompetent security guys.

"Hello fellas," Ellen greeted.

"Hello ma'am, we understand there was a break-in here last night and we want to check your security system to make sure everything is working properly."

"Yes, I was going to call you. Since someone broke in last night, I would say it is not working properly. Please come in and check it again."

They came inside and knew they had to work fast before Bradford showed up with the guy staying with her.

"Thanks, ma'am, we'll do our best to get to the bottom of this." The men opened the basement door and then said, maybe we should use the basement window. Ellen agreed that would be a better idea. Unbeknownst to them, Ellen had asked her neighbor, Tim, to put two of her security cameras down in the basement earlier. She downloaded the app and could watch what was going on down there. She paid for the subscription months ago and never had them hooked up.

"Well, before we tear up any more steps, where do you think we should look?" the one man asked the other.

"I have no idea. That fool Bradford would have us destroy every step to look for it."

This was interesting, Ellen thought. Bradford and these men were looking for something in her basement. She had no idea there was something down there of interest to anyone. She lived in the home for twenty-some years and the previous owners were deceased. She went to her filing cabinet. She couldn't remember the name of the people who were the original owners but she was sure she kept the paperwork.

As Bradford and Donovan drove around, Bradford began to get hungry. He pulled into a drive-thru and ordered a breakfast combo. "Anything for your friend?" the attendant asked.

"Oh, it's lights out for him. He had a rough night if you know what I mean," Bradford snickered.

Donovan started to wake up hearing him talk but he didn't let on that he was. He wanted to hear what Bradford was up to. He didn't expect him of any wrongdoing since he was a cop, but he thought it was interesting how quickly he got him out of the hospital. He acted as though he didn't want to be seen. Donovan thought he would have wanted to wait around for him to give his report to the police. Donovan wasn't aware of the two police officers who were admitted for their injuries at Ellen's or that would have made him more suspicious.

Bradford pulled into a parking space and got out his breakfast sandwich and hash brown. He was starved and needed food. He wanted to check in with the idiot brothers to see how they were making out at Ellen's. He could only keep driving Donovan around so long before he woke up and started asking questions.

Ellen was successful in her search for the deed for her home and the paperwork she filled out for the mortgage company. The previous owners' names were Helen and Victor Smith. She was hoping it would be Bradford and that would explain Officer Bradford's involvement with the two men in her basement. She searched her computer while watching and listening in on the two men. She keyed in their names to see what she could find. Nothing came up on the first search. Then, she put in Bradford after their names.

Boom – there it was!

The Smiths fostered a baby boy whose birth mother's name was Elizabeth Bradford! After finishing that article, there was another one. The boy was taken from the Smiths and put into a boarding school for troubled youth. The adoption process was started but was never completed. It appeared the Smiths were sad to have Brian taken away but it was either that or he could have ended up in a juvenile detention home according to an unnamed family source. They were devastated and never fostered or looked into adopting another child.

Another article appeared that was written after the Smiths passed away from an auto accident. Brian Bradford attended their funeral services and was never granted an inheritance. He said the Smiths considered him their son, and before Victor passed away, he said they took care of him in their will. However, according to the rest of the article, the will was never found and the attorney who drew it up was deceased. Ellen wondered if that had something to do with what the men downstairs were looking for. Just then, a knock on the kitchen door startled Ellen. Her computer screen still had the newspaper article pulled up, and when she answered the door, she found the two men from the basement.

"Your security system needs a little work," the one man advised. "Is it okay if we turn off the electricity now, ma'am?"

"Uh, yes, I guess," Ellen stammered. She didn't like the thought of her power being shut off since she had the security cameras on but then she remembered Tim asked for batteries for backup in case the power would ever go off so she wasn't concerned. "Just let me shut down my computer," she said, and then she saw her large screen displaying the information she was researching about Bradford. She hoped they hadn't notice.

The men walked outside and entered through the basement window. The one man did notice her computer screen. The other one said they better alert Bradford and get this taken care of quickly before she got any wiser.

Luckily, the cameras were working great and Ellen was able to see and hear everything they were saying and doing in the basement. She called the hospital and Donovan was already discharged. They said he left with a Brian Bradford a couple of hours ago. The next call she made was to Ben. She knew he was busy at the bakery but she didn't know who else she could trust. When she called, she asked him if he could leave and come to her house immediately. Ben could tell in Ellen's voice, it was urgent and he said he'd be right there. She was watching the camera as she spoke to him. They were using flashlights and she could hear them say they had to call Bradford if they didn't have any luck locating it.

They had to be looking for the will but why did Bradford think it was in her basement. And why did he wait all these years to begin searching for it? She wished she could have done more research before they turned the power off.

Ben pulled into her driveway and she was so glad he finally arrived. She needed to let him know what she found out. He was carrying a box from his bakery, and when she answered the door, he said, "I made some of the pastries Donovan likes. I thought he may be hungry when he gets home."

"Thanks, Ben, I know Donovan will appreciate it. Come on in and I'll get you a cup of coffee." They walked into her kitchen and she pointed down to her cell phone that was displaying the cameras in action. She had the volume turned down so the men wouldn't know what she was up to. Ben was shocked at what he saw. They were tearing her basement apart, and for what reason, he thought.

"Don't you think we should call the police?" he asked quietly.

She shook her head 'no' and asked him if he'd like to go out onto the patio since the electricity was off. The men heard the back door slam shut and were glad they were alone in the house. They took this opportunity to call Bradford and tell him they couldn't find the will or any legal document for that matter. Bradford said that his father always told him it was in a safe place and the basement was his work space. Bradford had already looked for it when he was able to get into the house last year when Ellen was away on one of her trips. They said they looked everywhere and now the basement is a total wreck.

"Keep looking," Bradford said. "If you want your share of the loot going to the pawn shop, you'll find it!" He said it a little too loud and turned around to see if Donovan was still passed out. Donovan heard everything but kept his eyes closed. He knew Ellen was in danger and he had to get back to her house to help.

Then Bradford asked, "What's that old lady doing now?" They told him she had company and was outside on the patio. Bradford answered, "Good, keep her out of the house if you can. Whoever is with her will hopefully keep her busy for a while. In the meantime, look anywhere you think my old man could have put a small safe box."

"Will do," the one man answered and hung up.

Ellen and Ben heard everything the men said. "Did you ever see anything in the house, Ellen?"

"No, but weren't you friends of the Smiths?" she asked.

"Yes, Victor and I went way back. I would think if there was a safe in the house, it would have been in one of the walls or a trap door in one of the rooms downstairs."

"That's a good idea, do you think you could help me find it while those two knuckleheads are tearing up the basement?"

"I'll be glad to. We just need to be careful, especially with your injury."

"I'm fine, let's get started before they realize what we're up to."

Ben and Ellen started their search using sunlight from the windows. Ben pulled up the living rug and didn't see any sign of a trap door. Then he looked in the dining room, parlor, and Ellen's office. There was one painting that was left behind from the Smiths that Ellen loved. She never moved it and all of a sudden, she asked Ben to look behind it. There was no safe in the wall. Just as he was putting it back, a piece of paper fell on the floor. It read:

'To whoever finds this, please show it to the police.'

On the other side was an affidavit that was signed by the Smiths and notarized. Ben quickly put the picture back on the wall and said they needed to leave immediately.

Donovan was hoping Bradford would get tired of riding around and go back to Ellen's. He seemed irritated that his buddies weren't coming up with the will he was looking for. Bradford started the car up and drove to a seedy hotel on the other end of town. It seemed he had been staying there and went into one of the rooms. Donovan waited to make sure he wasn't looking outside, and then he opened the back passenger door and slid out. His head throbbed but he had to get away. Luckily, he had his cell phone and when he tried to dial Ellen's number, he was pushed to the ground.

This time, he rolled over and kicked the man who has been causing so much chaos. Bradford fell to the ground in pain and Donovan quickly got up and called the police. He wasn't going to worry Ellen about this. He knew he had to get back to her place and was hoping for a ride with one of the officers.

The police arrived and Donovan told them what Bradford had been up to. They handcuffed him and put him in the back seat of one of the police cars, while another one drove him to Ellen's. Donovan desperately needed his prescription filled but wanted to take care of Ellen first. He had to make sure she was okay. Once they arrived, Ben met the officers at their patrol car and informed them of the situation. He didn't want them to fall going down the basement stairs and warned them that the power was turned off.

In the meantime, Ellen got up without her cane and hugged Donovan. She was so glad to see him and helped him onto a patio chair where they could both see the action going on out of harm's way. The two men in the basement were trying to reach Bradford when the officers snuck in and caught them off guard. They saw the destruction the two had made and immediately put them in cuffs.

As they were reading them their rights, the two men looked at Ellen and one of them said, "What did you do with the will, old lady?"

With that, Donovan, feeling bad or not, got up and punched the guy in the face and said, "That's from her, and don't you ever disrespect a lady again!"

The police officer ignored what he did and walked him out into his car along with his buddy who didn't make eye contact with Ellen or Donovan. After they were safely locked up in the patrol car, Ellen and Ben wanted to show them the note they found. The officers asked them if they could bring it down to the police station so their chief could see it and make out a report. On the way, they picked up Donovan's prescription as he insisted on going with them.

The chief read the note and was saddened by it. He was a good friend of the Smiths, and in the note, Victor said that he was writing it on his deathbed. He told how Brian had threatened to kill him and his wife, Elizabeth many times, and unfortunately, they thought he had changed when they sent him to the expensive boarding school. It seemed that Bradford asked for money the night of their car accident, and when they refused, he caused them to have the accident. Brian was driving on the wrong side of the road causing them to run off the highway and crash.

Unfortunately, Elizabeth died instantly and Victor died a few days later. He had his brother hide the note in the picture and was instructed to never read its contents so he didn't know anything about what had happened. His brother passed away a few years ago and he was the only next of kin Victor had.

The chief took down their report and Ellen had the saved camera video of the two men tearing apart her basement. "I think we have all the evidence we need, and I'll get your statement when you're feeling better," he said to Donovan. "I want to hear all about your joy ride," he said with a smile.

Ellen said she thought it was time to look for a new home and perhaps get a dog. She didn't feel safe living in that house any longer. Donovan agreed and said he would help her find a place when they got back from the cruise.

"Let's go help Amber," he said. "I think we both need a change of scenery."

Chapter 7

William and Katelyn were walking to their rental car when Katelyn's phone went off. "It's Ellen calling. She probably wants an update on Amber."

They got into the car as she answered. She put Ellen on speaker so they could both talk to her. "Hello, you two! How's Amber?" Katelyn and William took turns telling her about getting her an attorney and their next meeting.

"Would you like two more to help you?" she asked.

"Do you mean you and someone else?" William inquired.

"How about me?" Donovan teased.

"That would be awesome!" Katelyn was so excited to see them. Ellen didn't mention what had happened at her house as she didn't want to worry them. They decided to leave on the first flight the next day and were going to make reservations at the Hampshire Inn where Katelyn and William were staying.

Abby and Jim didn't see Katelyn or William at all yesterday. Katelyn called her last night and updated her on their visit to see Amber. Abby filled her in on her visit to the police station. Detective Miller finally reached her last night and they were going to meet him over at Weldon's place around ten o'clock in the morning. Katelyn thought it would be a good idea to tag along and called William to let him know.

Once they arrived at Weldon's, Katelyn was taken in by the beauty of his home and backyard. She was envious of his gorgeous flowering plants and manicured trees. He definitely had a gardener, she thought.

Abby waved them over as soon as she saw them. There was a small table set up with coffee and danishes. She was waiting to introduce them to Detective Miller as he wanted to go over the rules of their visit. As they walked over, Katelyn noticed all of the neighbors standing around outside and some had lawn chairs set up in their yards. William was amazed at the circus Abby's news report was creating.

"Katelyn and William, this is Detective Miller."

"Hello sir," William and Katelyn said together. After the detective filled them in on where they were allowed to go on the grounds, he quickly left to call in backup for crowd control. The news van was attracting more and more onlookers.

"Good morning Bedford Falls! I'm Abby Winters and I'm reporting from Hampshire, a small town in the fair state of New Hampshire!" The camera scanned around the backyard of Weldon's estate and then turned back to Abby. "We are here looking into the murder investigation of Weldon Hopper, a well-known mystery writer. With me is Detective Miller of the Hampshire Police Department." Jim focused the camera on Abby and the detective at this point.

"Detective Miller, what happened to Weldon Hopper?"

"Unfortunately, we don't know much at this time. His disappearance before the time of his death has led us to believe he was possibly injured before being killed."

"What was the extent of his injuries?" Abby questioned.

"That is confidential information that cannot be disclosed at this time."

"Detective Miller, there is an individual who was arrested in connection with Mr. Hopper's murder. What can you tell us about her involvement in this crime?"

"We did arrest a female suspect who the victim had a relationship with."

"What kind of relationship did they have?" Abby asked. She thought his answer made it sound as though they were more than just colleagues.

"As far as we know, they had an intimate relationship."

Katelyn looked at William and said, "That is absurd!" The crew around her hushed her, and she looked over at Abby and mouthed, "Sorry!"

Abby pushed on. "What information do you have that they had an intimate relationship, detective?"

"Well, we have our sources which we are not privy to discuss."

"In your opinion and that of your department's, is there any reason for the community to be worried about another attack?"

"No, we believe this was pre-mediated and no one in the community should be concerned about another such act."

"Detective, we noticed there haven't been any funeral arrangements made for the deceased. Is the investigation holding this up or was it requested by the family?"

"Our investigation is not holding up any funeral or memorial services. At this time, this is an active investigation into the death of a beloved member of our community. The department is doing its best to get to the bottom of this crime and bring justice to Mr. Hopper and his family. No further questions, please."

"There you have it, folks. We will continue to report on the murder investigation of Weldon Hopper, a well-known mystery author. We will be bringing you interviews from some of those who knew him best." With that, Abby signed off.

She then walked over to Katelyn and William with her eyes as wide as quarters. "Do you believe that Weldon and Amber were lovers?" she asked.

"No, this case is getting stranger by the minute," William answered. "It doesn't add up. In any murder investigation I've known of, especially after this much time has passed, more information has been disclosed to the public. It appears they are certain they have the killer but have no evidence connecting her. An email stating she could kill him on some days is not enough to go on. I'm suspicious of their whole investigation," William concluded.

"Let's see what the police report has to say," Katelyn added.

They left Weldon's, and William and Katelyn had a couple of hours before they were due to meet Attorney Bakersfield at one, so they decided to take a trip to the local library in town to look through old newspapers. There had to be something they were missing in Weldon's murder. They were hoping the newspapers that reported his death would lead them in the right direction.

"Good morning," William greeted the person behind the desk at the Hampshire Public Library.

"Good morning," she said half-asleep.

"We were hoping you could point us in the direction of the newspapers you have from the past two weeks."

"Sure, see that room over there? Go inside and sit down at one of the microfiche machines and someone should come in sooner or later."

"Thank you," and as they stepped away, Katelyn whispered, "Gee, she was helpful, and do you believe they still use microfiche machines?"

They both laughed out loud and William noticed they got a stare from another library employee who was putting returned books on the shelves. "Sorry," he whispered to her.

Inside the room, it was dark since no lights were on and only sunlight was coming in through the windows along the one wall. The woman who stared at them came into the room and asked what they were looking for. Her name was Sue and they introduced themselves. As soon as William began to speak, her mood lightened up. It seemed she liked his English accent, and immediately warmed up to them. He explained which editions they were looking for, and finally, she got out of them the reason.

"Oh, Mr. Hopper! What a dear man," she said. "He donated copies of all of his books to the library, visited the schools to educate our children on the importance of reading and education, and he would contribute to all of our fundraising events."

"Gee, he sounds like a great role model for your community. Why do you think anyone would want to kill him?" Katelyn asked.

"If you ask me, I think that spoiled rich girl they locked up did it or had someone else do it for her. The police don't have any other suspects, and all of the neighbors noticed her coming and going out of his house at all hours. I think she finally snapped and took it out on poor Mr. Hopper."

She helped them get started and said she would be around if they needed more help. The day Weldon was killed was a Wednesday so there were no articles in the morning paper. On Thursday, there was a photo of Weldon along with a news story on his death and a short blurb from the Police Chief. Friday's edition featured an article on Amber with a photo of her arrest. On Saturday, the reporter on the case must not have had any new information and stated that a memorial service was being planned for the following week but no details were given on the day or location. In the following days, nothing was reported. It was like it had become old news.

"This is so strange. They arrest someone for a murder and then the story is all but dropped. The police aren't looking into any other suspects; they just assume they have the murderer and are waiting for her trial."

Katelyn agreed with William. "When we meet with the attorney today, we have to find out his perspective and how he can help poor Amber. She may have unknowingly sent an email saying she could kill him at times but that doesn't mean she did it. They have no evidence except she was in the wrong place at the wrong time."

William shook his head. "Well, it seems like we are getting no information here that can be of help, so let's head on over to that little coffee shop we passed on the way."

"William, I'm kinda all coffeed out."

"As us Brits say, 'how about a spot of tea?'" Katelyn laughed as they started to stand up.

"Have you finished already?" Sue asked as she walked into the room.

William looked up and said, "Yes, it appears there weren't many articles written about Mr. Hopper."

"Yes, I think after that woman's arrest, the paper didn't have anything else to report."

"I'm surprised the police didn't continue their investigation," Katelyn said while putting away her notepad. "You never know, there could have been another person involved," she added.

"Well, they didn't see anyone else and there was talk of her having an accomplice but nothing was found."

"Sue, do you know when they had the memorial service?"

"As far as I know, it was supposed to be this week but I haven't heard any more about it. Maybe Weldon's family is going to take care of it."

"That's a possibility." William thanked Sue for the information and they headed out of the library.

***

Ellen and Donovan were on their way to New Hampshire and their flight was scheduled to arrive at three forty-five in the afternoon. William volunteered to pick them up so Katelyn and William had plenty of time until they needed to be at the airport since it was a short ride.

***

On their way to the coffee shop, Katelyn told William that she found it interesting that Sue thought Weldon's family was going to take care of planning a memorial service but he didn't have any family. "That's exactly what I was thinking, Katelyn. Let's go into the shop and see if we can start up a conversation with any of the regulars in there."

As they walked in, they thought they saw Sophia, Attorney Bakersfield's assistant seated at one of the booths. Her back was towards them and she didn't see them come in.

"Yeah, these two come in to set up an appointment for Alan to represent this guilty dame. The guy's dead and she's the one who did it, and they think he can prove her innocence. Do you believe it?"

How unprofessional, Katelyn thought. The nerve of her sitting here in front of everyone in the coffee shop talking about Amber like that. William was fuming and decided to be the better person and take a seat and cool off before speaking to her.

They sat down at a table near the door, and when she got up to leave, she walked past them. Her face turned a few shades of red as William stopped her.

"We will not be keeping our one o'clock appointment today. We will find another attorney whose office personnel do not find themselves entertaining others by discussing their cases. Please tell Attorney Bakersfield he can contact me if he has any questions regarding his dismissal. I will be glad to fill him in on the conversation you just had with the folks in the shop. Good day!"

After she left, they both burst out laughing. William played it cool and wasn't argumentative. Katelyn applauded him and said, "Now who are we going to get?"

William got out his phone and immediately started looking for a new attorney. "There's a guy on the other side of town, Derrick Harrison, who looks like a good chap. Let's get out of here and check him out." They got the tea they ordered to go and off they went. They didn't want to disappoint Amber today without having found an attorney.

They parked in the parking garage of a large office building complex and easily found the law office of Attorney Harrison. They made their way through to the elevator which took them to the third floor.

"His office should be down this corridor," William stated. They arrived as a middle-aged woman was unlocking the office.

"Hello, how are you?" the woman greeted with a smile.

"We're doing fine," William answered.

"Do you have an appointment to meet with Attorney Harrison?" she asked.

"No, unfortunately, we do not. We are from out-of-town and wondered if there's any chance he could meet with us?" The woman felt bad as they looked desperate but she knew her attorney's schedule was full for the next couple of weeks.

"Come on in," she suggested, "and we'll see what we can come up with."

Katelyn was glad to let William do the talking. Besides his English accent, women just loved him. "Fantastic," William replied.

The woman offered them water or coffee while she booted up her computer. "Nice day out; I hope it doesn't rain later," she remarked, working as fast as she could to log in.

"Agreed, where I'm from, it's been a bit rainy lately so I'm glad for the sunshine."

"I take it you're from England, correct?"

"Yes, ma'am, born and raised there as you Americans say." The woman laughed. William was putting on the charm which was just what they needed.

"Attorney Harrison's wife is from a small town in England."

"Well, I'll be," he answered. "Do you happen to know which part?"

At this time, Attorney Harrison arrived and greeted the woman as he walked past. "Which part of England is Charlotte from?" she asked.

"Worcestershire," he answered as he shot her a side glance wondering why she was asking.

Immediately, William spoke up. "I grew up in Worcestershire! That is amazing I come all the way across the pond and meet someone married to a fellow Brit from my village."

Derrick laughed and told him his wife's maiden name. As luck would have it, William knew Charlotte and she was a playmate of his sister's.

Attorney Harrison wanted to talk to him some more and asked why they were there. William briefly explained their connection to Amber and needed to find her legal representation as soon as possible.

"Edna, please see that if we have any cancellations, you put William and Katelyn in their spot." He then turned to them and said, "I'm sorry guys, I have a full schedule for the next couple of weeks and the only thing I can offer you is to meet with my new attorney, Michelle."

"How soon could we meet with her?" Katelyn inquired.

Edna looked at her schedule which was mainly wide open since she was just hired. "Let me see if Michelle has any time now," she said with a wink.

Michelle was thrilled to have her first client meeting. Harrison walked into her office beforehand and gave her a quick briefing on what he wanted her to find out. He knew this was going to be a high profiled case for their firm and didn't want anything to go wrong.

Ten minutes later, Michelle came into the reception area and introduced herself. Katelyn and William followed her down a narrow hallway to her office. It was obvious she recently decorated it and she had fresh flowers and plants throughout the room.

"Before we get started, can you tell me a little bit about yourselves?" she asked.

"Certainly," William began first. Michelle was very attentive and after they both finished, William asked her about herself. Michelle was a recent grad from Harvard Law School, and her father was Attorney Harrison's college roommate. The two men stayed close throughout the years and Michelle considered him an uncle.

"So, now that we got that out of the way, you probably want to know why we're here." Katelyn was in a hurry to get down to business. "Yes, I understand you would like Attorney Harrison to represent Amber Jenkins, who has been arrested for the murder of Weldon Hopper."

"Yes, that is correct. But she has been arrested unjustly and with no proof," Katelyn emphasized with a concerned look.

William looked at her as if to say, calm down and let me handle this. Katelyn took a sip from her water bottle as William filled her in on what they knew about the case. He also told her what happened at the café earlier. Michelle was shocked that Sophia, whom she had met at a town charity function the attorneys held, would discuss cases openly in public. She assured them that wouldn't happen in their office.

Michelle felt sorry for Amber after hearing what William had to say. If the woman was innocent, they were going to have to start looking into the investigation leading up to her arrest immediately. William's phone rang and he saw it was Attorney Bakersfield's office. He asked him why they cancelled their appointment today and William was more than happy to tell him. The attorney apologized for Sophia's actions and told him he would discuss the matter with her. He also said he had the police report and would be glad to share it with him and his new attorney. Michelle had been listening in and quickly jotted down her email address so it could be sent over. It finally appeared that things were moving along, Katelyn thought.

After he hung up, he asked Michelle if she would let them know when she received the report. She was going to give them a call and they could meet to discuss it. She was looking forward to digging into a case for Derrick. On their way out, Edna was away from her desk. They would thank her the next time they saw her.

About an hour later, Michelle called to let William and Katelyn know the report just came over. She had a meeting scheduled with Attorney Harrison at two o'clock and said she wanted to discuss it with him before they met. William pleaded with her to get them invited to the meeting. She said it was to go over all of the cases she's assisting him with but she'd do her best to see if they could join them for a few minutes while reviewing the police report. She called back fifteen minutes later and said it would be okay.

A few minutes before two o'clock, Katelyn and William walked into Attorney Harrison's office. They were anxious to get down to business and hoped the attorney would be willing to give them more time. "Good afternoon, Edna," William said as he took a seat.

"Good afternoon to you both," she replied. "I believe Michelle is on her way." Michelle saw them and escorted them into Attorney Harrison's office. It was huge and had more furniture than William's first flat.

"Thank you for seeing us, Attorney Harrison," Katelyn said as she shook his hand. William noticed the photos of Derrick's family and immediately recognized his wife.

"I see Charlotte is as lovely as ever," he remarked.

Derrick smiled and said, "I agree," as they took their seats and were ready to begin.

"Michelle and I both read the police report. It seems that a neighbor saw Miss Jenkins enter Mr. Hopper's home on the morning of the murder."

"That's impossible!" Katelyn blurted out. William again gave her a pleading look to stay calm.

William told them what happened according to Amber which she told the police. "I see that she stated she was trying to reach him and knocked on the doors and called him. The police couldn't find any missed calls on his phone."

"Impossible," William replied. "I can assure you that if she said she called him, she did."

"Michelle, do you know if the officers checked her phone for the calls she made that morning?"

"I will find out, Attorney Harrison."

"Please do."

"The report also shows she ran off into her car when she left."

"Women tend to do that when it's getting ready to rain," Katelyn said matter-of-factly.

William smiled and then asked, "Who was the neighbor who saw Amber go into Weldon's house?"

"We're going to have to request more information. Michelle, what's your schedule look like the rest of the week?"

She looked at him like 'what are you talking about', and answered, "I can be available to work on this case as much as you'd like."

"Good, then I'd like you to accompany them to meet with Miss Jenkins and start working on the case for me. Keep me informed of all the facts that you uncover, and I will make myself available for short meetings, such as this."

On their way out, Michelle walked them to the door and said, "Let's meet with Miss Jenkins tomorrow morning at nine o'clock. I'll try to come up with more information from the police. In the meantime, if you remember anything else, please let me know." She handed each of them one of her newly-printed business cards and she walked back into Derrick's office.

They finally felt like things were moving along.

"Well, what do you think?" Katelyn asked.

"I think we finally found Amber legal representation," William replied. They were anxious to go visit her and tell her about her new attorney.

When they arrived at the prison, they didn't mention to Amber what happened with Alan Bakersfield. Amber was having a rough time adjusting to life as an inmate. She knew William and Katelyn would be her best chance of getting released.

"We'll be back tomorrow with Michelle from Attorney Harrison's office. If you think of anything else that happened that morning, she'll need to know. By the way, do you know where your cell phone is?" William asked.

"Everything was taken from me when they brought me here. I assume they have it with my other personal items."

"Okay, we'll let Michelle know as it appears Weldon's phone doesn't show any missed calls from you that morning," William advised.

"That's strange, I called his cell a couple of times and even tried his house phone."

"Okay, don't you worry about a thing. We'll see what we can find out," Katelyn said as she held her hand up to the glass before they walked out. Their visiting time was up and they had to get to the airport.

Chapter 8

When they arrived at the airport, they were glad to see their dear friends again. William and Katelyn were concerned about Ellen's leg, noticing she was using a cane. She assured them that it was healing fine and her doctor said to only use it when she's standing or walking for long periods of time. Then Donovan began filling them in on the mystery at Ellen's. They couldn't believe anyone would go to such lengths looking for a piece of paper and were glad the men responsible were caught.

Abby wanted to join them but they thought it was best if the news van didn't show up. Jim reminded her of a conference call with their boss at four, so they had to stay behind. Abby was hopeful that some of the folks in the community would start to talk so she'd have more stories to report on. If not, she was certain they would be reassigned some other news stories to follow.

On their way to the Hampshire Inn, William and Katelyn took turns filling them in on what they knew so far about Amber's arrest. It floored them when they heard the police and a neighbor said that Weldon and Amber were lovers. Ellen thought that was the furthest thing from the truth.

"There's no way Amber and Weldon were having an affair." Donovan added, "I think that if they knew them, they would realize it was more of a father-daughter type relationship. He was a mentor to her."

They all agreed they had their work cut out for them. Clearing Amber in this town was going to be a challenge. They just hoped they could get to the bottom of it before Amber spent too much time behind bars.

They arrived at the inn and realized it had been a long day for Ellen. They decided to let her rest in her room while the rest of them would try to get some answers. Someone had to know something. Ellen was happy to relax for a little while and they promised they would wake her before dinner. No one was hungry yet and they decided to grab something later. As soon as Ellen laid down, she immediately fell asleep.

The others decided to meet in Katelyn's room and go over everything they knew. Donovan wondered if the attorney, Michelle Jackson came up with anything yet and they decided to call her. She told them about her telephone call to the police station and the meeting she scheduled with one of the arresting officers for this evening. They asked if they could join her in meeting him, and she reluctantly agreed. She didn't want to scare off the detective but they all knew Amber and Weldon so she thought it could be helpful. After all, this was a murder investigation. Michelle said she would ask the detective to meet her at the inn, and hopefully, he would be okay with them joining their meeting. They asked her if she had time, to join them before he arrived.

William asked the front desk if they could use the conference room next to the business office for a short meeting. Everyone assembled there waiting for Michelle's arrival. Katelyn made the introductions and Donovan thanked Michelle as he shook her hand.

"Nice to meet all of you," Michelle began. Once they all got seated, she began to fill them in on what she found out from the police, which wasn't much. The others told her about Amber's relationship with Weldon and how absurd it was to think they had any type of romantic relationship.

It was getting late and Michelle received a call from the police department informing her that the detective was out working on a case, and unfortunately, had to cancel their meeting for this evening. After she informed the others, they wondered if he was busy or if this was just an excuse.

The next morning, Michelle left Attorney Harrison's office and was anxious for her first meeting with Amber. Derrick trusted her and she wanted to make him proud and prove he made the right decision in hiring her. She was going to go to the prison with the letter Derrick instructed Edna to prepare for her. In it, he stated Michelle was there from his law firm representing Miss Jenkins. Once she made it inside, she was going to meet with Amber along with William and Katelyn. After getting her statement, she needed to look at Amber's cell phone and see what information she could retrieve from it. Michelle was going to get the telephone company to send over the call log. She thought it was exciting to be working on a real case after all of the ones the professors made up in class for them to solve. Unfortunately, this case involved a real human being who was in prison, someone who was murdered, and a possible suspect on the run, and who knew what else. Michelle knew she was going to have her hands full.

Katelyn and William were waiting for her arrival. They walked through security and were glad she was finally going to meet with Amber. Michelle grabbed her legal pad and pen out of her briefcase. She forgot her iPad and was going to have to take notes the old fashion way. She put in a request for Amber's personal belongings and wanted to get as much information that she could to work on. Amber met them in a small conference room, and after she came in, Michelle introduced herself and gave her one of her business cards.

Her small box of belongings was delivered as they were getting ready to start. Amber explained everything that had happened that morning. She didn't remember seeing anyone around and said the only neighbor who could see into Weldon's backyard was the next-door neighbors. She didn't know them but Weldon had some choice words with them one day when she was over. They were complaining about his one tree that bordered the fence between their yards. They said it needed to be trimmed and Weldon disagreed. He later said they could take him to court if they didn't like it.

Michelle asked for her passcode for her cell phone. It needed to be charged and Amber told her who her service provider was for receiving the call log. Amber thought it was odd that Weldon's phone didn't show any missed calls from her. Michelle said she would meet with her again tomorrow morning after she did a little digging. She wanted to stop by and meet with one of the detectives who arrested her. Michelle was curious as to what he would have to say.

At the police station, Michelle found out that Detective Miller was the senior detective in the arrest of Amber. She knew that was the name of the detective who couldn't meet with her last night. He was in Sergeant Reynolds' office discussing their plans for an upcoming fishing trip.

The front desk officer told them an attorney named Michelle Jackson from Derrick Harrison's office was there to see Detective Miller regarding Amber Jenkins. The detective felt bad that he couldn't meet with her last night but the sergeant didn't know they had a meeting scheduled. The sergeant got up and closed the door.

"Well, it looks like Derrick's got his nose in this one," the sergeant sneered.

Detective Miller wondered why he said that and got up to go meet with her. The sergeant didn't appear too happy about an attorney showing up to look into their investigation. "Leave it to me," the sergeant instructed, "I'll go out there and get rid of her."

"That's not necessary," the detective advised.

"Just stay put until I get rid of her." The sergeant opened and closed the door behind him.

What's gotten into him, the detective thought as he scanned through his emails on his cell phone.

The sergeant walked out and introduced himself to Michelle. She was confused as the arresting officer's name was Detective Miller. "What can I do for you, Miss..."

"It's Jackson," Michelle stated as she handed him her business card. "I was hoping to speak to Detective Miller if he's available."

"Oh, I'm sorry, he's out on a call. What can I do for you?"

"Well, I wanted to discuss the details surrounding the arrest of Amber Jenkins."

"I see, I'm very familiar with the case. It's sad that it came to this. I understand that she went berserk. Something about them being lovers and her finding out about an affair he had. Sad, very sad."

"Where did you get the information that Weldon had an affair?" Michelle questioned. "I met with Miss Jenkins this morning and she never brought it up."

The sergeant chuckled. "Miss Jackson, do you think she would admit to killing him over his infidelity? I don't think so."

"What evidence do you have that he was involved with another woman or women?"

Michelle didn't like the way the sergeant was acting. She realized she needed to talk to Detective Miller who arrested Amber. Talking to this guy was getting her nowhere. She finally thanked him for his time and he walked away. She glanced around the lobby and saw photos hanging of the officers. She saw one that had Detective Andrew Miller's name underneath it.

She casually asked the officer who just relieved the other officer at the front desk if Detective Miller would be back soon. "Oh, I just saw him in the sergeant's office. He'll probably be out soon," he replied.

The sergeant walked back into his office and told Detective Miller he just got rid of her. The detective left and was still surprised that the sergeant wouldn't let him meet with her. He wondered what was up with that.

Michelle noticed the detective leaving the office and quickly jotted down a message for him on the back of one of her business cards. She asked the front desk officer if she could use the restroom. She walked down the hallway and saw he was waiting for a cup of coffee to finish brewing. Other officers were around, and as she walked by him, she shoved her card into the palm of his left hand. He looked up and saw her. She smiled, and as she left, he read the note.

'Hi, I'm Michelle Jackson and I'd like to arrange another meeting with you. Please call my cell as soon as you can.'

He flipped the card over and saw her number. He walked back to his desk and told his partner, Stan, that he had to run an errand and would be back soon. Stan waved him off as they were catching up on paperwork.

As soon as he got into his car, he dialed Michelle's number. "Thank you for calling me, detective. As you know, I would like to arrange another meeting to discuss the arrest of Amber Jenkins. My firm has been hired to represent her. I know you couldn't make our meeting last night and I was hoping we could reschedule."

She deserved that and he was curious why the sergeant wouldn't let him meet with her. He wasn't his supervisor but he was definitely throwing his weight around regarding this case.

"Yes, I can meet you at four o'clock this afternoon," he replied.

"Great, do you want to meet in my office or somewhere else?"

"Your office will be fine," he said as he jotted down the address before hanging up. In the meantime, he wanted to do a little investigating to find out why the sergeant was acting so strangely.

Michelle was anxious to get back to her office to charge Amber's cell phone and to call her service provider. She was on hold forever and had to hang up for her meeting with Derrick. He had some time in between appointments and wanted to find out about her discussion with Amber. She brought him up to speed on the meeting with her and the visit she had at the police station.

Derrick was surprised that the sergeant didn't want her to speak to the arresting officer on the case. He was glad Michelle set up a meeting with the detective that afternoon. "Great job, Michelle. Let me know if I can be of any help," he offered as he left her office.

She thought the cell phone should be charged and tried to power it on but with no success. This is strange, she thought. It had been on the charger for two hours so it should have been charged although she was so busy after talking to the detective and updating Derrick, maybe she didn't have it plugged in properly. She checked the connection and plugged it in again. In the meantime, she called Amber's cell phone provider again.

This time, she wasn't going to hang up.

At three forty-five, Katelyn, William, and Donovan arrived at Attorney Harrison's office. Edna led them into the conference room while they waited for Michelle and the detective. At four o'clock, Edna called Michelle to let her know Detective Miller had arrived. Edna brought him back to her office so Michelle could meet with him privately. She wanted to explain that the others were there so he wouldn't feel ambushed.

"Good afternoon, Detective Miller."

"Please call me Drew."

"Since I spoke to you, I wanted to let you know that a few of Amber's author friends arrived in town. They requested to meet with me and were hoping they could join us to shed some light on the relationship she had with Weldon."

"That's fine, let's get started." Drew wondered if any of them were famous like Weldon as he walked down the hallway to meet them.

"Everyone, this is Detective Andrew Miller."

He looked around the room and saw William Blackwell, the famous mystery author from London. He was thrilled inside but had to keep his cool. He shook their hands and found an empty chair next to Katelyn's.

"Well, I think it's time to get started," Michelle said as she logged into her iPad. "What can you tell us about the day Amber Jenkins was arrested?" she asked.

Drew informed them of the next-door neighbor seeing her enter Weldon's home and never seeing Weldon alive afterwards.

"What other proof do you have that she did it?" Katelyn asked.

"There was evidence on her computer that she wanted to kill Weldon."

"Are you referring to the email she sent to all of us, detective?" Donovan questioned.

"Uh, yes, and..."

"Detective, you do realize when people are upset with another person, they may use the expression, 'I could just kill them.'"

"I realize that, but we do have a witness seeing Amber run off after the time of Weldon's death."

"And who are these witnesses and why aren't they coming forward? An innocent woman was charged with murder and it appears the police stopped their investigation and poor Amber is stuck in a jail cell awaiting trial." William summed up what they all were thinking.

Before Drew could reply, Michelle filled everyone in on a conversation she had with the sergeant earlier.

"Tell me, Drew, doesn't it appear strange that your department's sergeant said you were out working on a case when you were sitting in his office? Furthermore, why would he lie to an attorney representing someone you arrested? Isn't there a strict code protecting the citizens of the state of New Hampshire?" Katelyn asked.

This lady is tough, Drew thought, but she had a point. He was as perplexed as they were regarding Sergeant Reynolds' behavior.

"Okay, okay," Drew stood up and looked around the room. "I understand everything you are saying and I think it's time we get down to business. Tell me everything you know about Amber Jenkins and Weldon Hopper."

The group told him what they knew about their relationship, and how her father was a dear friend of Weldon's. They grew closer after last year's murder mystery weekend at the Winchester Estate and found out recently that they were collaborating on a new mystery together. Ellen had mentioned to Donovan that she felt Weldon had something bothering him lately but he never told her what it was. She figured in time if he needed someone to talk to, he'd open up.

Michelle excused herself to go get Amber's cell phone out of her office. When she came back, she tried to power it on. Again, not working. Donovan asked to take a look at it. They continued talking while he started to open the back of the phone.

"Do you think it got damaged, mate?" William asked.

"No, it looks like the SIM card is missing," Donovan replied.

"That's strange if it's been in storage at the police station," Michelle said looking at Drew. Drew assured them that no one had access to the property room unless an officer was approved.

"And who gives this approval?" Katelyn asked.

"Well, usually the Chief of Police or someone from the District Attorney's office," Drew answered reluctantly. He knew what they were all thinking. The sergeant was hiding information. That couldn't be, he thought. He never knew Reynolds to be the type to do anything, not by the book. What was he up to? Drew needed answers and had to find out.

They decided to meet again tomorrow after Drew got off duty, and in the meantime, find out as much information as they could. They wanted Drew to try to solve the mystery involving the sergeant's actions and the cell phone, and they were going to speak to Amber. If she was using the cell phone the day of Weldon's murder, someone removed the SIM card and the police were the only ones who had access to it. This was strange, Drew thought. He had to get some answers.

Especially if they arrested the wrong person.

Michelle walked everyone out and told Edna that she would probably need to use the conference room beginning at four o'clock each day for the next two weeks. She wasn't sure what they were going to dig up but wanted to continue meeting with Drew and the others. She knew what the detective was thinking; there's something suspicious about this investigation and she hoped he would be able to get to the bottom of it.

When they got back to the inn, they updated Ellen on what they found out. She wanted to go with them to the next meeting and was anxious to help in any way she could. Katelyn called Abby to let her know Ellen and Donovan were staying at the inn.

"I can't wait to see them! Let's get together for dinner!" Abby said excitedly.

"As long as you don't have a camera crew and start interviewing my friends!" Katelyn replied.

"You think I would do that? Give me some credit!" Abby stated. Katelyn told her to meet them in the restaurant next door to the inn and they were planning to have a quiet dinner there. Abby invited Jim but he wanted to stay in and order room service and watch the game that was being televised.

The group gathered in the bar area of the restaurant waiting for Abby. "You did tell her we wanted a quiet and relaxing dinner, correct?" Donovan joked. Katelyn laughed with the rest of them. They all knew she could be a little much to handle. Just as they were ordering drinks from the bartender, she arrived.

"Hi guys," she greeted. "It's so good to see all of you!"

They all hugged her and the hostess was ready to seat them. After catching up, they placed their orders and were ready to get down to business. William looked around the room to see if anyone was paying attention to their conversation before he started. He filled them in on what they knew. Ellen thought the sergeant was hiding something and the fact that he may have been the one responsible for the cell phone tampering didn't look good. Abby was worried that Amber was being framed and the police were involved.

"Do you think you can trust this detective who you are working with?" she asked. "Particularly because he was the one who arrested her," she added.

"Well, he's all we got and if he's willing to do some snooping around the police station, at least we have someone on the inside. Let's hope he can come up with something," William replied.

They mentioned their meeting the next day with Michelle and Drew, and immediately knew they shouldn't have. "I want to come!" Abby said. "I know Amber and Weldon, too!"

Oh, gee, why did you have to say this in front of her, Katelyn thought as she looked at Donovan. "Okay, on one condition, young lady. You come alone, no cameras, no news report on anything we find out, and you stay quiet."

"Donovan, what kind of person do you think I am?" she asked.

"Just a good friend trying to help out," Ellen answered for him. "We just need to keep this on the lowdown since the detective is trying to find out if there's anything suspicious going on down at the precinct."

"Got it," Abby said in a serious tone.

Chapter 9

The next morning, Katelyn heard a knock at her door. She figured it was one of three people: Ellen, William, or Donovan. She called out, "I'm coming," and when she opened the door, no one was there. She closed it and a minute or two later, she heard another knock. She didn't know if someone was playing tricks on her but she opened it again. This time she discovered a note that was taped to her door.

'You are looking in all the wrong places for answers. I will contact you again soon to meet. Keep your eyes open and be careful who you trust.'

Uh no, Katelyn thought as she read the note, again. It felt like she was reliving the Winchester Estate incident. At least it didn't tell her to meet them, whoever this person was 'alone.' There would be no way she'd fall for that again, she thought.

Just then, William came walking up and saw her standing in the doorway. "Whatcha got there?" She pulled him inside in case anyone was watching. She showed him the note.

"What do you make of it?" she asked.

"It looks like we got ourselves a deep throat."

"Or a killer after me!" she exclaimed.

"You don't know that but I think we need to keep this between ourselves, Katelyn. Besides, do you believe that a deep throat would want to hurt you? Maybe he knows what's going on with the bobbies."

"William, what are bobbies?"

"Sorry about that. I forgot I wasn't in London. That's what we call the police."

"I wonder how soon he or she will want to meet." Katelyn didn't like the thought of having a secret informant contacting her.

"Well, we'll do what the note says and keep our eyes open and wait for the next message. I'll be with you if you have a meeting with deep throat," he reassured her.

"I'll have to think about it," Katelyn said, grabbing her purse.

They walked down to the breakfast buffet that was set up for all the guests. She kept looking around wondering if this deep throat person who wanted to meet her, was in the room. As soon as they arrived, Ellen and Donovan waved them over to their table. They were just being served coffee and juice, and the server took their beverage order.

"How are you doing this morning?" Ellen asked cheerfully.

Katelyn tried to remove the worried look off of her face but didn't do a very good job. Ellen immediately knew something was wrong and remembered she left her cell phone in her room. "Dear, do you mind going back to my room with me? I forgot my phone and I better get it. You never know when you'll miss an important call," she added.

"Sure," Katelyn got up and assisted her back to her first-floor room.

"Okay, what's going on?" Ellen asked as she closed her door.

"What do you mean?"

"Katelyn Winters, you know part of my job as a mystery writer is sniffing out things and I smell a rat."

"How about a deep throat for starters?" Katelyn asked her. After reading the note, Ellen said this may be the break they have been looking for to clear Amber of Weldon's murder.

"Katelyn and Ellen have been gone a while," William mentioned while looking at his watch. "I better call to see if they're okay."

"Instead of calling, why don't we just walk down to her room. It's only a short walk," Donovan suggested. They still had plenty of time before their nine o'clock meeting at the prison so William called the server over who was going to put a reserved sign on their table for them to use when they returned.

William knocked on the door, and immediately said it was them so they wouldn't be worried about anyone else. He knew Katelyn was concerned about deep throat. "Just a minute," Ellen called and Katelyn opened the door for them to come in.

"What's going on, ladies?" Donovan asked.

"Oh, just some girl talk, nothing to be concerned about." Ellen wasn't too convincing, and William looked at Katelyn's concerned face.

"You told her, didn't you?" he asked.

"Told her what?" Donovan said feeling totally out of the loop.

"Yes, she did and I'm glad," Ellen answered.

"Sit down, Donovan, we got ourselves another mystery to solve. This time it involves a deep throat." Katelyn pulled out the note and showed it to him.

"What do you make of it, chap?" William wanted his thoughts before he said anything.

"It seems this deep throat may want to help us."

Donovan and Ellen agreed with him while Katelyn was on the fence. "I think you're feeling this way because of the kidnapping last year, which we all understand," Ellen said, trying to reassure her that everything was going to be okay.

They decided to go back down to the breakfast buffet and while they were there, try to strike up a conversation with as many people as possible. They didn't know what deep throat looked like but they assumed it was a hotel guest or employee. As they made their way around the room, they met a lot of families who were in town for a wedding. They ran into a couple of businessmen and women who were attending a conference at the hotel. No one appeared to be anyone other than who they said they were.

It was nine-thirty and they decided to arrive at the prison a few minutes early before visiting Amber and were glad Michelle was there as well. They wanted to show her the message Katelyn received and find out what she thought of it. This case keeps getting stranger, Michelle thought. She recommended they wait until they met with Drew at four o'clock for his input. She advised that they should not mention it to Amber. Ellen argued that they should share it with her as she may have some idea as to who sent it. Michelle finally relented and they went inside and were escorted to the same conference room they had used yesterday.

"What do you make of it?" Michelle asked after Katelyn showed Amber the note.

"I have no clue," she replied. "Do you think someone has information and wants to help me?" she asked.

"That's what it appears to be," Katelyn said, putting the paper away.

"Did you by any chance recognize the handwriting?" Michelle figured it wasn't a possibility but felt compelled to ask.

"No, I'm sorry, I don't."

Michelle heard her cell phone buzzing in her purse and accidentally pulled out Amber's. "Oh, Amber, we discovered your SIM card was missing from your phone," Donovan mentioned.

"I never removed my SIM card; where is my phone?" she asked.

"It's right here," Michelle said pointing to it. She had just found hers but was too late to answer it. She was concerned about what Amber had just said. "You mean this isn't your cell phone?"

"No, mine has a rose-colored case on the back of it." They looked the case over and it was a solid blue. "This looks exactly like Weldon's phone," she replied.

They could see Amber was tearing up and Donovan added, "I know we'll get to the bottom of this. We have all solved much more difficult mysteries in our books, haven't we?"

That made Amber feel better and put a small grin on her face. Everyone said their goodbyes and Ellen said they'd be back tomorrow. William told her to keep her chin up and was certain this would soon be over. Amber thanked them for coming and for helping her. Michelle patted Amber's shoulder and told her to stay positive.

Michelle saw the missed call from an unknown number. She excused herself and said she would see them at four o'clock in her office. She asked them all to keep her informed if they hear anything else.

Once she got into her car, she took her cell phone out of her purse and decided to listen to the voice message before leaving the parking lot. It was from Drew:

'Hey Michelle, can you and I meet before the four o'clock meeting today? I can get away for lunch at eleven thirty if you have time. Give me a call back at this number. Thanks.'

Michelle looked at the time and realized it was already eleven o'clock. She quickly returned his call and he answered on the first ring. He wanted to meet privately and asked if she could meet him at his home. He lived in a small community a few miles away. She agreed and decided to check in with Edna and then drive over to Drew's.

At eleven-thirty, Drew pulled into his driveway. He waved to Michelle who was parked across the street. She met him at his door and they quickly went inside. He had some information and wanted to see if Michelle was able to find anything out.

He began, "It seems there was a mix-up in the property room the day that Amber was arrested. Her belongings were put inside someone else's box and the person whose belongings were in Amber's box is deceased."

"Who is this other person who's deceased?" Michelle was afraid to ask.

"That's where it gets tricky. The other person is Weldon Hopper."

"What, how can that be? He wasn't arrested so how did his things get put in Amber's box?"

"That's the million-dollar question that I'm trying to find the answer to. It was tough enough to get this information without causing suspicion."

"But you were the arresting officer, you should be able to get the facts."

"True, but some lips are sealed and between you and me, things are not adding up. I'm not pointing any fingers, but I think we need to be careful who we talk to."

"Agreed," Michelle said and showed him the photo she took of the note Katelyn received on her hotel room door.

"I think things are about to change," Drew remarked.

"We have to work together on this and no secrets," she emphasized. "I'll trust you unless you give me a reason not to," she added.

"You got it. I'll be in your office at four and I'll try to keep digging."

Michelle left and was anxious to get back to the office. She wondered what happened to Amber's phone if Weldon's was put in her box. Why would a deceased person's cell phone be mistakenly put inside the personal belongings of a person accused of their murder? Drew was right; things just weren't adding up.

Derrick didn't have time to meet with Michelle in the afternoon but she was so involved in trying to figure out what she knew so far in this case that she didn't mind. She wanted to see if she could find out any information before the four o'clock meeting. She was certain they were missing something, but what? She went into the conference room and decided to use the whiteboard to jot down everything they knew. She started with Weldon, then Amber, the next-door neighbor, and Sergeant Reynolds. She was reluctant to write down deep throat since the others didn't know she mentioned him to Drew. Then she wrote underneath their names what clues they had. She figured when the others arrived, she could add to it whatever they had. It would make things easier to see a visual of everything they knew.

Drew was the first one to arrive for the four o'clock meeting. Edna escorted him back to the conference room and shortly after, the others arrived. Abby was running late and was going to be there around four-thirty.

They all walked into the conference room and were surprised to see Michelle's list. They sat down and waited to hear from Drew and Michelle. Michelle was the first to address everyone. She explained the information on the whiteboard and asked them for anything else that should be included. They didn't have too much to contribute as they already told Michelle pretty much everything they knew.

Drew advised everyone that he had some news but he wanted to make sure whatever was shared wasn't leaving the room. They all agreed and he told them about the property room mix-up the day Amber was taken into custody.

"How could that have happened?" William asked.

"How long did it take them to discover the mistake and where is Amber's cell phone now?" Ellen questioned.

"These are all good questions to which I am trying to find the answers. You have to realize what I am dealing with. I have a sergeant who is acting a little out of the ordinary, and if I ask too many questions, I may jeopardize what we're working on."

"So, what do we do in the meantime?" Katelyn asked.

"We lay low and do what we have been doing. We investigate quietly and wait for the opportunity to present itself. Now, I understand you have been contacted by an unknown source who may have information. We need to proceed cautiously."

"Hold on, you know about deep throat?" Katelyn looked over at Michelle as if she was betrayed.

"Well, I think it's about time we include him in our investigation. No secrets, okay?"

William, Ellen, and Donovan shook their heads in agreement, and Katelyn looked him straight in the eye and said, "That includes you, too."

Drew shook his head and said, "I agree, and everything stays between all of us in this room."

Just then, Edna knocked on the door and said, "There's a Miss Abby Winters here to join you."

Drew asked, "Is she the news reporter I met over at Weldon Hopper's house the other day?"

"The one and only who so happens to be Katelyn's sister," William replied. "What is she doing here?" and before anyone could respond, Abby came rushing through the door.

"Sorry I'm late, did I miss anything?"

Drew looked at Katelyn, surprised at what he just learned. "Well, I got to be going now. I'll see myself out," and headed for the door.

Michelle was just as surprised as he was and followed him. "Drew, I'm so sorry. I didn't know Katelyn's sister was a reporter. Let me handle this."

"See that you do. I can get into a lot of trouble at the precinct as it is without having a nosy reporter involved in this."

"Okay, I'll call you tomorrow," and Michelle walked back into the conference room. It wasn't going as planned, that's for sure, she thought.

Michelle had to break the news to them without hurting Abby's feelings. She explained that her presence in these meetings made the detective uncomfortable sharing information as he is working undercover. She would be able to cover the story once there was any news to report, but at this time, any media coverage would be detrimental to the investigation. She told Abby she hoped she understood and to give them time to figure this out. Abby said she did and wanted to be the first reporter notified when there was any news to report. Michelle agreed, and Abby left.

"Wow, she took that rather well," William noted.

"Yes, I think our little Abby is growing up," Ellen said with a smile.

Katelyn knew Abby too well. She wasn't at all happy and she didn't look forward to her questions after every meeting they had. But for now, she knew she had to concentrate on helping Amber.

After they left the office, they headed back to the inn. They were all going to meet with Amber in the morning and Michelle was going to contact Drew. She knew he was their only hope at the police station. She was wondering who this deep throat was. Was it someone she knew? She hoped this person would contact Katelyn with more information soon.

"Well, it's about time you got back," Abby informed Katelyn when she got inside her hotel room.

"How did you get in here?" Katelyn asked, bewildered as she hadn't given her a key.

"I'm your celebrity sister, girl. People just love me! Now tell me everything I missed."

Katelyn told her that under no circumstances was she going to risk helping Amber by discussing the investigation with her. After a while, Abby reluctantly said she understood and reminded Katelyn that she was going to be the first reporter on the scene broadcasting any news coverage. In the meantime, Abby decided to focus on the people in the town for news reports. Katelyn was happy that she decided to take a different angle.

Abby and Katelyn talked until around nine o'clock, and after she left, Katelyn decided to go down to the gym inside the hotel. It had been another long day and she wanted to work out before showering. She hadn't had a chance to check out the fitness center since they arrived. Afterwards, a nice, long hot shower would relax her and the water would soothe her aching muscles before going to bed. No one was there when she entered the gym. To obtain entry, you had to use your room card so she felt safe. She put in her earbuds to listen to some of her favorite workout songs.

She was there for around fifteen minutes when a man entered. He was filling his plastic refillable water bottle, and when he saw her, he smiled and said 'hello.' Katelyn was rowing at the time, and she thought it was strange that he took the machine next to hers. There were only two rowing machines in the room and she thought no more about it. She rowed for fifteen minutes and decided to use her least favorite machine – the ab cruncher. She reset the weights and began. She looked up once and saw the guy was looking over at her. He smiled and looked away. She was starting to get the creeps and wished someone else was in the gym.

She wondered what William or Donovan were doing. She took her cell phone out of her pocket and was going to send them a text. Clumsily, after she typed the message, her phone fell out of her hand. The guy quickly walked over to pick it up for her. She wasn't able to get it before him as it bounced away from her when she dropped it. She didn't want him to see her unsent message but it was too late. He retrieved it, and as he was walking toward her, it was evident he read it. She regretted calling the guy strange and worried that he could be a creep.

He said, "Here you go," and Katelyn mumbled, "Thanks," and pushed the phone back into her pocket without sending it.

She decided to leave before it got any stranger. She had her fill of water and decided to walk down to the reception area where they had coffee and tea set up for the guests. She thought a nice cup of tea would taste good after her shower. As she was leaving, the guy from the gym appeared. He walked over to the coffee station as she was walking out. He watched her leave before he left.

She hurried back to her room at record speed. She had to be careful not to spill her tea, and when she got there, she fumbled with her room key. Gee, she thought, what's up with my coordination today. She opened the door and quickly closed and locked it. She decided to sit down at the table and drink her tea. She needed to calm down. It was just a coincidence that the guy showed up in both places. She turned the shower on and let the water soak in. After a good night's sleep, she would realize she was being silly, she thought.

Chapter 10

The next morning, Katelyn called Ellen to see if she was ready to go down for breakfast. She said she was and Katelyn told her she'd be by in a few minutes. As she walked out, she saw another note was taped to her door. She looked around and didn't see anyone. She stuffed it into her purse and decided to go meet Ellen and then read it once they were all together.

"Good morning, Ellen, how are you feeling today?"

"I'm doing great, so much better. Are you hungry?" Katelyn lied and said she was. In the pit of her stomach, she felt sick. She didn't know who deep throat was, and the strange guy from the gym last night worried her. She tried to seem upbeat as they walked down to meet William and Donovan.

"Hello, hello, my fair ladies," Donovan greeted. William and Donovan were already there and grabbed a table. He hugged them both and William put his arm around Katelyn. He could tell by looking at her face that something was wrong.

She whispered, "I got another note this morning."

"What did it say?" he asked.

"I don't know, I just got it as I was leaving." William motioned for Donovan to stay with Ellen while they walked outside to the rental car. "Okay, let's see what deep throat has to say today." William could see Katelyn was emotional and he wanted to read it first. It read:

'You need to step up your investigation before it's too late. Remember to watch who you trust. I will be in touch later today.'

"Who do you think we shouldn't trust? I wish he would be direct and tell us something!" This was all starting to take a toll on Katelyn.

"I know, it's like he's playing a game with us," William agreed.

Just then, Donovan was standing outside the car. William hit the unlock and he asked them what they were doing. William handed him the note. "What do you make of it, chap?"

"Another meaningless note. At least he said he would be in touch later today."

"I don't like this," Katelyn added. "To think that someone picked me out of the blue to send these messages to is…"

William patted her hand. "Hey, we're going to find out what's going on sooner or later. Don't worry, we're going to be with you all day and all night so you don't have to worry about a thing."

She told them about the guy from last night. They said if she saw him again, to let them know. Thinking that they were gone too long and didn't want to worry Ellen, they walked back into the dining area. Katelyn wanted to get some fruit and yogurt as it was going to be another long day.

After breakfast, they piled into the rental car and were going to meet with Amber and Michelle. They decided to fill Ellen in on the latest note Katelyn received this morning.

When they met up with Michelle, she said she didn't have much to report, and Katelyn showed her the note. "This is good news, guys. We may get what we need from this unknown source today."

"True," Ellen added, "but why be so mysterious?"

Michelle thought about it and said, "You guys are mystery writers. Maybe deep throat is doing this to make you work harder to solve the mystery."

"The only problem is, he's not giving us any clues," Katelyn lamented.

By this time, they were in the small conference room at the jail, and Amber was escorted in. They continued their conversation hoping they could figure something out. "Let's start over with our suspects." As Michelle jotted down everyone's ideas on the whiteboard, she began drawing lines to link the suspects together.

For example, Sergeant Reynolds worked with the guy in the property room. They found out from Drew that his name was Ed. They continued working around the board, and after they were finished, Michelle took a photo of it on her cell phone before erasing it. They didn't have much to go on. They needed Drew's help to find out why Amber's belongings were put in a box that was supposed to be Weldon's. It didn't make sense. Ellen asked if she should go down to the precinct and try to get some information. She could pretend to be a distant relative of Weldon's and since she knew him the longest, had the most background information on him.

It was worth a shot, they all agreed.

After saying goodbye to Amber, who was feeling useless being locked up, they assured her they would be back again tomorrow. She had tears in her eyes as she waved goodbye to her dear friends.

"Okay, let's get a plan in order before Ellen and I go into the precinct," Donovan instructed.

"Who said anything about you joining me?"

"You didn't think I would let you go in there alone, did you?" he replied.

Since Ellen and Donovan never met the sergeant, everyone agreed it was a good idea. Before Michelle left, she sent Drew a text letting him know what they were planning to do so he wouldn't be caught off guard. He wasn't sure if it was a good idea but thought it was worth a shot. He would be working at his desk so he would be there when they arrived. Donovan was going to grab an Uber and they would meet up with the others afterwards.

Upon entering the precinct, Donovan held Ellen's arm as if she needed more assistance than she did. Her legs were doing fine, but he didn't think a little sympathy from the officers would hurt. They walked up to the front desk and she told the officer on duty in a weak voice that she was Weldon Hopper's cousin, who just flew in. She appeared distraught and asked if she could meet with someone to get the details of his death. The officer told them they could take a seat, and he would check to see if the sergeant was available. After he walked away, Drew passed by to let them know he was nearby. The officer returned and said the sergeant would be with them shortly.

The sergeant came out and introduced himself and extended his condolences to Ellen and Donovan. He led them down to his office where they could speak in private. "Thank you, Sergeant Reynolds, for seeing us," Ellen began as she wiped away some tears.

"Certainly, Miss..."

"Please call me Eileen." She didn't want to use her real name for obvious reasons.

"Eileen, I'm not sure what information you've been told about Weldon's death."

"Please, sergeant, start at the beginning if you may be so kind."

The sergeant elaborated on the story that had been circulating. When he got to the part where Amber supposedly entered the house, she asked him, "How did she kill him?"

The sergeant shook his head. "Unfortunately, poor Weldon's body was so disfigured that we're not sure how he died."

This was news to them. "You mean, after all this time the cause of death hasn't been determined yet?" she asked as she was overwhelmed by this.

"Yes, ma'am, we're not sure how Miss Jenkins did it and she's not talking."

Ellen and Donovan looked at each other, shocked by what they just heard. "Did you ever think someone else may have done it, sergeant?"

"We have witnesses who saw Miss Jenkins enter the house before the murder." Ellen didn't want to press her luck by asking any more questions about it.

"I would like to have Weldon's belongings that were removed from his house." They were interested in getting the cell phone and anything else that could give them some clues. Deep throat was not being helpful with his coy messages.

"Just a minute," and he left his office. Donovan looked over at Ellen, still not believing that someone physically hurt Weldon, possibly before he was murdered. Who would do such a thing? Five minutes or so later, the sergeant walked in with Drew and his partner, Stan.

"Eileen, I would like you to meet the arresting officers who have been working on the case. Unfortunately, there was a slight problem in the property room where we hold the personal items of suspects, and it appears Weldon's articles got mixed up with someone else's."

"Why would Weldon's items be put into the property room where suspects' items were kept?" Donovan asked. "The personal items that were confiscated should be returned to his family."

"Agreed," Drew replied. "We will make it a priority to find out where Mr. Hopper's belongings are. I'm sure the family would like to have them," he added.

"Thank you, detective," Ellen said through sobs.

After they left, Stan told Drew that there was no way they were going to find anything of Weldon's. "What do you mean?" Drew was floored that Stan felt this way.

"The sarge doesn't want anyone snooping around this case for some reason. He pulled Ed off the job for a few days after the murder."

"Ed, who works in the property room?" Drew asked, afraid of the answer.

"Yep, and after he came back, things were in such disarray, Ed told me that he had a heck of a time sorting everything out that the bozo who filled in for him created."

"Did he know who it was?" Drew was becoming more and more upset.

"No, some guy from another precinct. We didn't have any cases that week, so I never actually met the guy."

"Stan, I promised Weldon's family that we would make finding his belongings a priority so we need to do just that."

About this time, the sergeant walked over to Drew's desk and overheard what he just said. "Aw, don't worry about keeping a promise to a little old lady. She doesn't understand how busy we are and how these things happen from time to time. How about you guys take an early lunch, on me?"

Now Drew was concerned. The sergeant wanted them to leave for some reason, just like he pushed Ed into taking an unplanned vacation. "No sarge, I have plans for a late lunch today," Drew said. "Maybe some other time." The sergeant walked away.

Things weren't adding up and Drew didn't like it.

Drew stayed at his desk the rest of the morning. He sent Michelle a text about what happened this morning between Ellen and the sergeant. He wanted her to look into finding out what happened to Weldon's things. Michelle had a brief meeting with Derrick and updated him on what they discovered. He agreed that the police had to produce Weldon's things and asked Edna to prepare an official request from his office. She told Drew she would be by to see Sargeant Reynolds at one o'clock.

The sergeant went to lunch at eleven thirty and at twelve-thirty, he walked back into his office. While he was gone, Drew and Stan met with Ed to find out what he knew about his replacement that week. He had little information as the guy came in after he left, and from what he understood, no one got to know much about him while he was there.

"The guy kept to himself, and none of the officers had much to say about him. When I asked the sarge where they found him, he laughed and said he came highly recommended."

They looked inside the box with Weldon's name on it and only saw a few items. "Where did they put all the stuff they took out of his house the day of the murder?" Drew asked.

"Yeah, they took his computer and a lot of techy stuff," Stan added. Stan was a good guy but saying 'techy stuff,' really, Drew thought.

"I never saw anything like that," Ed replied. "Since the guy was murdered, I'm not even sure why I wound up with his stuff."

"Yeah, this whole thing doesn't make sense. Let us know if you find anything else," Drew said as he thanked him.

When Michelle arrived, she glanced over at Drew and was glad to see he was there. She marched up to the front desk officer on duty and asked to see Sergeant Reynolds. The sergeant didn't answer his phone so the officer decided to go back to his office. When he saw he wasn't there, he paged him. Drew looked at Stan and they both thought the same thing. The sergeant was down in the property room. They both jumped up and went to see what was going on. In the meantime, Michelle took a seat and sent Drew a text. He didn't have time to see who was texting him; he hoped his instincts were wrong and the sergeant wasn't involved in any dirty business.

When they arrived, Ed was on his computer playing a game. It seemed it was his lunch hour. "Did you see Sergeant Reynolds?" Stan asked out of breath.

"Yeah, he's in there," he pointed to the normally locked up room where the personal items were kept. Ed hit the unlock button so they could enter. He didn't like people bugging him when he was at lunch.

As soon as the door flew open, there was the sergeant. He was looking through several boxes on the table. "Hey sarge, someone's here to see you," Stan advised. The sergeant's face was beet red.

"What are you doing?" Drew asked.

"Well, ever since that knucklehead of a nephew of mine mixed everything up, now I'm trying to figure out what goes in each of these boxes."

"You mean Ed's replacement was a relative of yours?" Drew questioned.

"Yeah, he was planning on going to the academy but after he left this place in such a shambles, I told him there was no way I'd write a letter of recommendation for him."

"So, you don't think no one was hiding evidence, sarge?" Stan asked.

"No way, not on my watch."

They felt relieved that there was no dirty business going on. "How about we help you clear up this mess," Drew offered. "You go and meet with the person who's waiting to see you and we'll see if we can straighten this out."

"Thanks, guys, and can we keep this between ourselves? I don't want to lose my job and pension over that fool of a nephew of mine."

After he left, Drew read the message from Michelle. He texted her that the sergeant was on his way to meet with her and that they're in the property room trying to sort out the items. He asked her to take it easy on him and he'd explain later.

They started looking through all the boxes marked for the week of Weldon's murder. There was a log sheet that showed what was brought in for each suspect. Why Weldon's things were brought here was a mystery. And what happened to his computer? They were going to tear this place apart and upside down if they had to. They needed to find the answers to clear Amber's name.

***

The sergeant apologized to Michelle, and from Drew's text, she knew there was a problem. He said they were working on finding Weldon's personal belongings and would be glad to show her as soon as everything was in order. She accepted his explanation knowing that Drew was involved and was most likely, on top of it.

***

Earlier, Katelyn and William received a text from Donovan that he and Ellen had just left the precinct and were on their way back to the inn. Michelle was going to meet with the sergeant at one o'clock. It was already after two and they were going to meet in Michelle's office at four o'clock. In the meantime, Katelyn wanted to go back to the Hampshire Inn to make sure deep throat didn't leave her any more messages. When they arrived, nothing was taped to her door. They caught up with Ellen and Donovan and decided to go down and grab a cup of coffee to go over what they knew. While they were there, the guy from the gym walked in. He didn't notice them right away as they were seated on the far side of the dining area. When he saw Katelyn, he put his hand up and waved. She reciprocated and under her breath, she told William who he was. Upon hearing that, he told her to ask him to join them.

She stood up and said, "Hello, how are you?" He looked surprised that she was talking to him and answered that he just finished up his workout. "Would you care to join me and my friends?"

He looked over at the others and said, "Sure," and followed her to their table. It turned out his name was Brad and he was there for his sister's wedding. Since he had just broken up with his girlfriend, he decided to spend a few extra days away from home.

"And where might that be?" William asked.

"I'm from a small town in Virginia."

Katelyn spoke up before thinking. "My next mystery is taking place in Virginia!"

"So that's why you look so familiar!" he realized. "My sister loves mysteries and I've seen your photo on the backs of some of her books."

Katelyn beamed with pride.

"Is that why you were staring at her last night?" William joked.

Brad blushed and said, "That and she seems like a nice person." They all laughed and made plans to meet up at the bar later that night.

After leaving the dining area, William went with Katelyn to see if any messages were on her door. Nothing. Donovan and Ellen went back to her room as he wanted to keep an eye on her. When they arrived, Donovan sat down on the sofa while Ellen freshened up. A few minutes after they arrived, a knock was heard at the door. Donovan got up to answer it as Ellen was still in the bathroom. As soon as he opened the door, he saw it – a note taped to Ellen's door. He quickly opened it as his name was scrawled across the outside envelope. It read:

'You are getting closer. Meet me in the men's locker room tonight at ten o'clock.'

He stuffed the note into his pocket. No need to get Ellen concerned. He was surprised that he received the note instead of Katelyn. And whoever it was knew he was in Ellen's room. Someone was watching them, but who? He decided to meet with William before the four o'clock meeting to see what he made of it.

He sent William a text to stop by his room. Donovan told Ellen he'd come back to get her when they were ready to leave. William had already left Katelyn's room and when he saw Donovan's text, he immediately left to go meet him. On his way, he ran into Brad and they briefly exchanged pleasantries. He seemed like a good chap, William thought as he continued on his walk to Donovan's room. After he arrived, Donovan showed him the note. They both thought it was odd that it was addressed to him but taped to Ellen's door.

"Do you think we have a stalker on our hands? We don't even know who this deep throat character is. And this hotel is so outdated, they don't even have any security cameras," Donovan remarked.

"The fact is, you received the note so maybe deep throat thinks whatever you did today was leading us in the right direction. We have to discuss this with Michelle and Drew today."

Donovan agreed. "Let's go get Ellen and Katelyn and head over to Michelle's office."

Once they arrived, Michelle led the way into the conference room. Drew was on time, and after he arrived, Derrick joined them. He wanted to see what they found out, if anything, since his last update from Michelle. Drew began and told them what had happened at the precinct. He left out the part that the sergeant was doing his nephew a favor by letting him work for a week in the property room. He felt embarrassed for the sergeant and didn't want to make matters worse. He assured them that he and his partner were doing everything they could to get things in order.

Next, Donovan pulled out the note he received and read its contents. Michelle immediately jumped into action to write down everything Donovan did on the whiteboard. He detailed everything from the moment he left the inn until they arrived back.

"Did you see or talk to anyone else today?"

"No, I said 'good morning', or 'hello' to some people at the hotel and probably when we went to see Amber and at the precinct, but it was nothing out of the ordinary. Wait, there was this guy I saw on the street begging today. I felt sorry for him and handed him some money."

"What time was that?" Michelle asked.

"It was before we went to visit Amber."

"That's interesting, did he say anything to you?" Derrick asked.

"Just the normal 'thank you' type of remark. I don't think he is involved in any of this. He just appeared to be an older man in need of help."

"Let's keep an eye out for him tomorrow when we go to see Amber."

They agreed that meeting deep throat may be dangerous but Donovan and William insisted they could handle it. Drew said he and Stan could be in unmarked cars and stake out the parking lot as soon as it got dark and they could listen in on their conversation with deep throat through their cell phones. Ellen didn't like it but knew this was their only lead. Besides, if deep throat was a threat, why wouldn't he have done something already instead of leaving these notes?

William and Donovan decided to leave their rooms at nine-thirty, grab a quick drink at the bar with the ladies and Brad. They were going to excuse themselves before ten o'clock so they would be ready to meet deep throat.

When they got there, Brad was enjoying himself and ordered them all a drink on him. They listened to his story about how his girlfriend broke his heart. The guys excused themselves and said they had an errand to run and would return shortly. Brad seemed not to care and they continued to talk about themselves. He got up to go to the restroom but left his cell phone on the table. Katelyn couldn't help but look at it when a message popped up. It read:

'Thanks for keeping them busy. I'll take it from here and let you know when to meet me back at the room. This shouldn't take long.'

Katelyn wanted to tell Ellen what she read but Brad was already walking back to the table. She didn't know what to do. She wanted to warn them that she thought they were being set up by someone Brad knew. How could she warn them without looking suspicious?

Ellen suspected something was up. She noticed Katelyn reading the message on Brad's phone and decided she would pretend she was feeling sick. "Ever since I had the accident, my legs get cramps and I have to lay down. I hope you don't mind if Katelyn takes me back to my room."

Katelyn gave Ellen a concerned look and immediately jumped up to help her get up. "I'm so sorry, Brad, but I better see that she gets back to her room. Maybe we can join you another time."

"Sure," Brad agreed. "I'll look forward to it." After they left, he noticed the message on his cell phone. He wondered if they saw the message and that's why they left.

It was ten o'clock and Donovan and William had their cell phones dialed into Drew and Michelle's. Deep throat was right on time. He wore a long black robe with a hood and was carrying a small box. He motioned for them to sit down on the bench in the unlit section of the locker room. They did as they were instructed. He stood a few feet away. They tried to take in as much information as they could about his appearance.

Then he spoke: "Gentlemen if you want to find out what happened to Weldon Hopper and clear Amber Jenkins, you will find the answers inside this box."

"Why all the mystery?" Donovan asked.

"And how was Donovan on the right track today?" William added.

"Can you tell us something that will help us?" Deep throat laid the box down on the bench and walked swiftly away. He did it so quickly, there was no time for Drew and Stan to get there in time. Donovan and William wanted to grab him and pull off his robe but decided to check out the clues in the box. Michelle asked what was inside it. As they opened it up, they found a book; they searched the pages for any clues written down or highlighted in the text. No luck.

"Do you think he wants us to read this book for whatever answers he's referring to?" Donovan was irritated as he hoped deep throat would tell them directly what they needed to know. William thought they should take the box back to Ellen's and see what she and Katelyn made of it.

They were on their way to her room when they ran into Brad. "Hey Brad, sorry we had to run off so soon."

"No problem, I'll be around for a few more days. Maybe we'll see each other again."

He noticed they had the box and knew it was over. He headed back to the room he shared with his buddy who was waiting for him. Drew and Stan didn't want to blow their cover and told them to call them once they got to Ellen's room. Michelle said she would hang up and they could call her with any information they found out. She was glad Drew and Stan were involved.

As soon as the guys knocked on Ellen's door, Katelyn answered. They walked over to the small table and put the box on top. The book was new and as soon as Ellen saw it, she figured it was the one Weldon and Amber were working on.

"How do you think deep throat got a copy of a book that's not even published yet?" Katelyn asked.

"From what Weldon told me, they had quite a few chapters left to write, and then off to the editing phase."

"This is very odd; hopefully, Amber will have an idea as to how anyone got a hold of it."

"Ellen, deep throat said the answers we are looking for to clear Amber are in this book. I think someone needs to get started on it."

"I agree, William, and I'll be glad to start reading, especially since I'm sick."

Donovan and William looked at her and she explained the reason she gave Brad for leaving the bar early. They thought the text message he received meant that he was involved with deep throat and decided to keep up their conversations with him but had to be careful that he didn't suspect anything since they didn't know who they were dealing with. Drew and Stan were going to watch out for anything at the precinct and continue their work in the property room. After they left, Drew called Michelle and filled her in on their discussion.

Ellen couldn't sleep. She picked up the book and started reading. It was dedicated to Amber's father. She was anxious to see what the story was about. She started reading but her eyes grew heavy and before she knew it, she drifted asleep.

Chapter 11

The next morning, Katelyn picked up some coffee and breakfast items from the buffet and went to Ellen's room. She wanted her to stay in her room and didn't want Brad to see her moving around. She ran into Donovan and William and they were going to hang out in the dining area in case he showed up.

After having no luck in seeing Brad, William texted Katelyn to let her know they were heading down to Ellen's room. They didn't have to knock as Katelyn was waiting for them outside in the corridor. They entered the room and found Ellen deeply engrossed in the book. They all wanted to ask her if she found any clues but knew it was probably too early. They were getting ready to go meet Amber and suggested that Ellen stay in her room and continue reading. Katelyn was going to meet with Abby since they haven't spent much time together.

At the jail, William and Donovan were planning on asking Amber if she knew what deep throat was talking about. Drew and Michelle were going to be there as well. They took off at eight-thirty so they would have time to park and get through security. As they passed the diner near the prison, Donovan saw the man on the street begging again.

He automatically reached into his pocket and pulled out a bill. The man spoke softly and said, "Thank you, kind sir."

It suddenly dawned on him that those were the same words he had said yesterday. Donovan looked at the man. His face was dirty, badly in need of a shave, a baseball cap on top of his head and he wore filthy clothes. He felt sad for someone like him down on his luck. He wished he could have done more.

"Come on, Donovan, we're going to be late," William said as he dropped a bill into the man's cup.

Michelle and Drew showed up as they brought Amber into the conference room. They told her about the book that deep throat said would have the answers to clear her name. She was shocked that the book she was collaborating on with Weldon was published since it wasn't finished yet. She didn't know who could have gotten their hands on it. They advised her that Ellen is reading the book and they hoped to have some clues that would help them get her out soon. They also mentioned the guy who seemed to be working with deep throat and they were going to keep their eyes open for anything that seemed out of the ordinary. In the meantime, Drew said he and his partner were sorting through the boxes at the precinct and hoped they could find Weldon's belongings. Amber thanked everyone for believing in her. She felt more confident that with their help, things would get better soon.

Ellen was through the first three chapters and the plot involved a man who was searching for his past. He lived alone and had the occasional visitor or friend who would stop by. The man was a little rough around the edges, much like Weldon. She began the fourth chapter when she heard someone at her door. Thinking it was the maid service, she said they could come in. After a couple of minutes, no one entered her room so she got up to investigate. No one was there and she found a note taped to her door. She quickly closed it and locked the door. It read:

'Ellen, you need to finish the book to solve the mystery. Just keep your eyes open and look for the clues.'

Ellen reread the note and decided a cup of tea would help her stay focused. She gathered up her purse and headed down to the dining area. She thought about everything she had read so far but the note said she had to finish the book to find the answers. She was tempted to jump to the back of the book but was afraid if she did, she'd miss something. No, she decided to keep on reading.

After she finished her tea, she was getting up to go back to her room when Brad walked in. It appeared he had been at the gym and asked her how she was feeling. She told him much better and then he asked if she would like to join him in a cup of coffee or tea. Ellen decided to stick around in case she could get any information out of him. Besides, they were in a public place and people were around. They took a seat facing the front where new guests were checking in.

"Where are your friends?" he asked.

"Oh, they're around. I wanted to stay at the inn to rest a little after what happened to my legs last night."

"I don't blame you. I was hoping to see you alone."

"You were?" she asked surprised. "And why is that?"

"I think we have a mutual friend who would like to see you."

"I'm afraid I don't understand how we could have a mutual friend when you live so far away from me." She was getting scared and wished she had never run into him.

"Don't be concerned, Ellen, I know who you are."

Now Ellen was frightened. Was this guy some kind of nut or was he working with someone out to get her? She couldn't imagine what was going on.

Brad picked up his phone and sent a text. While he did that, Ellen made a run for it, even though her legs couldn't move that fast. She unlocked her door and deadbolted it. She quickly dialed Donovan's number and told him about the note and her meeting with Brad. He told her to stay put and he was on his way. Drew overheard the conversation and said he'd be in his unmarked car to assist in any way he could.

He hoped that this Brad wasn't a danger to Ellen or anyone else.

Donovan and William just left the meeting with Amber and walked past the beggar outside of the diner. There was something about the sad look in his eyes that made them feel sorry for him.

"Where are you staying at?" Donovan asked. The man pointed to the park bench across the street. "Here's some money, get yourself a hotel room and a nice warm bath and meal tonight."

Again, the man said, "Thank you, kind sir." They hurried to get into their car and return to the inn.

Drew was wearing a long-sleeved shirt and jeans. He wanted to fit in as a guest at the inn. He circled the common areas, the gym, the bar, the dining area, and looked around the pool. No sign of anyone matching Brad's description. Donovan and William went directly to Ellen's room and found her with Katelyn, quite shaken up.

"I don't know why he wanted to meet me alone or who this person is that is a mutual friend."

"Ellen, I think you need to calm down. We're not going to leave you alone. Do you think you feel well enough to continue reading the book?" Donovan asked.

"Yes, I'm not leaving this room until I finish it, and hopefully, find out the answers we are looking for."

"Good, and Ellen, for the time being, I want to stay with you in your room," Katelyn advised. "These rooms are huge and I think we'd both feel better being together."

Just then, Drew had an idea. "Since Ellen has been getting the recent messages from deep throat, how about you move down to Katelyn's room?" Drew suggested. "We can use your room as a sort of command center," he added.

"That sounds like a great idea," William said.

"Good, when the coast is clear, let's take the items that Ellen needs over to Katelyn's room."

"Okay, Drew, let's do it!" Donovan wasn't going to be as worried about Ellen if she stayed with Katelyn.

Ellen put the items she needed into a bag. She was going to go back to her room the next day to get whatever else she needed. With the book under her arm, she was safely tucked away in Katelyn's room. Luckily, they didn't run into anyone on the way. Once she got inside, she made herself comfortable and picked up where she left off in the book. She found it to be quite interesting but still, she couldn't find any clues. She hoped she wasn't missing anything.

They decided to have Michelle stop by the inn's bar at six o'clock for a drink instead of meeting in her office at four o'clock. They thought if Brad showed up, maybe they would be able to get some information out of him. Michelle was an attractive young woman and they knew how he felt about Katelyn. They didn't want to put any added stress on Ellen and told her to stay in her room and Katelyn asked Abby to come over and stay with her. Drew was going to be in the command center he set up in Ellen's room. Everything seemed to be in place.

At five-thirty, William and Donovan grabbed a table at the bar. They wanted to make sure they had a table instead of sitting on bar stools. Katelyn came down as soon as Abby arrived, and Michelle was there precisely at six. They knew if Brad saw the girls, he would want to join them. Drew had his earpiece listening in on their conversation. He took a walk down by Katelyn's room to make sure no messages were left on her door. He didn't see anything and made his way back to Ellen's room.

He heard Donovan say, "Hey Brad, care to join us?"

Brad was too far away for Drew to hear his reply. As he got closer, he heard Brad say, "Nice to see you all."

They introduced their friend, Michelle, and you could tell he was quite taken with her.

"Is Ellen feeling bad again?" he asked.

"Yes, just a little tired, but I'm sure she'll be okay," Katelyn remarked.

A little while later, they noticed Brad was texting someone. "How's your sister and the rest of your family doing?" Donovan asked.

"Huh, uh, okay I guess." His answer seemed strange since he said he was in town for his sister's wedding.

"That's good, weddings can be stressful," Katelyn added looking over at William.

The server came over and took their drink orders. They had to be careful how to proceed but they needed answers if he had any. "What type of work do you do, Brad?"

"I work for my father's marketing business," he replied.

"That sounds like an interesting job," Michelle remarked. "Do you do commercials or print ad marketing?" she asked.

"A little bit of this and that mostly for locally owned businesses."

"I can imagine you work a lot of long days," William said.

"Yes, it can be."

They could tell he didn't want to talk about it and they dropped it. Brad was receiving an incoming call and excused himself to the nearby hallway to take it. Donovan decided to take this opportunity to get up and use the restroom in hopes that he could hear a portion of Brad's conversation.

Brad had his back turned to him and Donovan heard him say, "I understand but the old lady isn't here. I'm not sure if she told them anything. Yes, I know, I'll do my best." He hung up and turned around and faced Donovan.

"Okay, I think now you and I need to talk."

Brad looked sheepish and Donovan was glad Drew was listening in on his cell phone. "What do you want to talk about?" Brad asked.

"I need to know who you're talking to about Ellen and what you know."

Brad knew it was a lost cause and he was going to have to come up with something. "Tell you what, meet me back at my room 302 in a half-hour. I'll tell you what I know."

"Okay, but no games," Donovan warned him.

"No games," and Brad headed back to his room.

When Donovan arrived at the bar, he told them that he was meeting Brad in less than thirty minutes in his room. William insisted on joining him and Drew was going to be listening in. Michelle went with Katelyn back to her room to wait until the meeting was over.

Ellen found herself intrigued by the book. She must have read close to two hundred pages when Katelyn and Michelle arrived back at the room. The lonely man in the story was being stalked by a man who claimed to be his brother. His father never spoke of him having a sibling let alone a brother, and the man was being tormented by this so-called relative. He was receiving threatening letters in the mail demanding very large sums of money.

Could this be the clue, Ellen wondered. She continued reading.

It was time for Donovan and William to meet with Brad. William dialed Drew's number so he would be ready in case they needed help. Donovan knocked on the door and Brad answered. He let them in and there was a strange eeriness in the room. They couldn't put their finger on it.

"Thanks for coming," Brad said as he motioned for them to sit down.

"What information do you have for us?" William asked.

"Nothing like getting right down to business, eh?" Brad said with a laugh. Neither Donovan nor William found it amusing and Brad began. "I'm not here for my sister's wedding."

"We kind of figured that out," William answered. "Why are you here?" he asked.

"I'm here because I was hired to look into a murder investigation," he answered.

"Whose murder are you investigating?" Donovan asked.

"Weldon Hopper's," he replied. He noticed their facial expressions which told him they weren't surprised.

"Who hired you?" William asked.

"Well, for now, that's strictly confidential. I will tell you that things are not what they seem."

"Do you believe Amber Jenkins killed Mr. Hopper?" Donovan was hoping for at least an answer to that question.

"Well, if I was a betting man..." Just then Brad's cell phone rang. He said he had to take the call and he would catch up with them later. They left and went back to join Katelyn and Ellen.

Just then, Ellen finished the book. It seemed that the man was locked away in the hidden wine cellar in his home. Ellen wondered if Weldon had such a cellar and told Katelyn, who immediately sent a text to Drew. Drew grabbed his jacket and hopped in his unmarked patrol car. He was calling in for backup, and then Stan called. He apprised him of the situation and said he would meet him there.

Once they arrived, Drew grabbed his weapon. He hoped he didn't need to use it. Stan was already there and ready to go inside. The house had been vacant since Weldon's murder. They opened the door and walked inside. If Weldon had a wine cellar, it would most likely be downstairs. They took out their pistols and slowly walked down the carpeted stairs. They reached the bottom of the steps and looked around. They didn't see anything resembling a wine cellar and decided to start opening doors, being careful in case anyone was around. After they checked each room in the basement, they decided to continue their search upstairs. They checked the door to the room closest to the upstairs kitchen. It looked like a pantry and when they went inside, they discovered another door. They opened it and were surprised to find what they were looking for. The wine bottles were all lined up according to their types.

They noticed another door inside of it that was locked.

"I wonder what Weldon kept in there," Stan asked.

All of a sudden they heard a muffled noise. It sounded like a weak animal in distress. Drew said, "Let's knock it down," and with that, both officers kicked the door in.

There they found a weak man, lying on the cold tiled floor. They didn't know who he was or how long he'd been there. Drew immediately called for an ambulance. He realized the man must have been in there for days and it

146

didn't look good. He saw a lot of items that he thought were missing from the precinct in Weldon Hopper's investigation.

The paramedics arrived and took the man's vitals. They discovered that he may not have much time so they rushed him to the Hampshire Hospital. Drew informed Michelle and the others what they found. In the meantime, backup arrived and they began their investigation.

Drew was deep in thought. Who was the man locked up in Weldon's wine room? And who was deep throat? Did Brad have any involvement in all of this? They needed answers and hoped the man would survive to tell his story.

Michelle met Drew and Stan at the hospital. They didn't know if the man had been reported missing or had any family. They wondered if he had something to do with Weldon's murder. Why were the computer and other items they saw being taken out of Weldon's house the day of his murder inside the wine room? They didn't know who was responsible or who could help them. Deep throat did warn them to be careful who they trusted. They hoped deep throat would make another appearance. They needed his help.

While they were waiting to hear how the man was doing, Drew and Michelle walked outside to his car. They wanted to check in with the others who were in Katelyn's room and let them know about their discovery.

"Deep throat told Ellen the answers we were looking for were in the book. If she wouldn't have read it, we wouldn't have known about the man locked up in Weldon's wine room. Ellen, were there any other clues that were mentioned in the book?" Katelyn asked.

Ellen thought for a few moments and said, "The lonely man knew he didn't have a brother but this person claimed to be his long-lost brother and was threatening to blackmail him. He wanted very large sums of money. So, he hired a private investigator to find out who this blackmailer was."

"Brad just told us he's a private investigator and was hired by someone to look into Weldon's murder," William reported.

"That's interesting," Michelle added.

"In the book, was the lonely man famous that this guy was after?" Drew asked.

"Yes, very wealthy and lived a very luxurious lifestyle. He was very kind and donated to many charities."

"Very kind, did it say that in the book?" Donovan asked.

"Why yes, several times. Why?"

"A man is begging every day outside of the jail when we go to see Amber. I'll give him some money and he always replies, 'Thank you, kind sir.' I wonder if that's a coincidence," Donovan said.

"I think tomorrow we need to check this guy out," Drew added.

"No problem, I'll do what I've been doing and try to get him to talk."

"Good, in the meantime, everyone, stay safe and call if you see or hear anything else. Stan and I will be hanging out at the hospital."

The rest of the night was quiet. When William and Donovan walked back to their rooms, they were hoping to run into Brad. They did a quick look around the bar and gym but they didn't see him. Katelyn and Ellen decided to go to bed early hoping that tomorrow would bring the answers they were looking for.

Chapter 12

"*Detectives, the man* is awake," a nurse called out to Drew and Stan.

It was morning, and they spent an uncomfortable night sleeping in the well-worn waiting room chairs. They jumped up and immediately walked down to the man's room. He had a breathing mask on and they were giving him fluids intravenously and he looked up when he saw them. He seemed to recognize them but it couldn't be possible.

"Hello sir," Drew greeted.

They introduced themselves and sat down next to his bed. They wanted to speak to him in a calm normal tone. Not wanting to scare him as they didn't know what he had been through. "Sir, can you tell us your name, please?"

He started to mumble something but it didn't make any sense. "Would it be easier if you wrote down your answers, sir?" Stan offered.

The man seemed irritated and didn't want to talk or write. His monitor went off and started beeping loudly. A nurse ran in and told them they had to leave. The man closed his eyes. They hoped they didn't upset him too much.

They decided to go home, take showers, and check in at the precinct. They didn't have to be at work but if they heard anything about this case, they were going to be available.

At ten to nine, William and Donovan were walking to the jail. Donovan had a bill in hand ready to give the man on the street. They didn't see him. They looked around and wondered if he was in the diner. They peeked in and didn't see him so Donovan decided to go inside and ask one of the servers. "No, I know who you mean but I haven't seen him today. He's usually here early and I always sneak him out a cup of coffee and a donut."

"That's very kind of you," Donovan told her.

"That's what he always tells me," she remarked. "I hope he's okay," she added.

"If you see him, can you ask him to call me?" Donovan asked. "I want to help him."

"Sure thing," she walked away putting Donovan's business card in her pocket.

They had a lot of information to pass along to Amber. She was shocked to hear about the book Ellen received that they were writing. She advised them again that the book was nowhere near finished let alone published. She was surprised to hear they found a man in Weldon's wine room. She had no idea who he was. She felt like a failure, sitting alone in a jail cell and not able to come up with any information to help free herself.

After they left the conference room, Michelle said they could meet in her office or at the inn for their afternoon meeting. It was up to them where they wanted to meet, especially if they found anything out, and she was going to see what she could find out about the items that were found at Weldon's house last night. She couldn't believe his computer and other items were carried out of his house and then returned later. Who would have done this? Hopefully, Drew could find out.

Donovan was in a hurry to look for the man outside of the diner. He told William he was going to hang around in case he showed up soon. William was going to head back to the inn and check up on Katelyn and Ellen. He wanted to try to find Brad since they didn't finish their conversation last night. He hoped he could shed some light on the person who hired him.

Donovan walked around outside, looking down the busy streets and didn't see him. There was a narrow alley on the left side of the diner. He decided to walk down there before going back inside. He started down and didn't see anyone. The kitchen window was cracked open and he heard the normal chatter between the cooks and the servers. He was just about to turn around when he saw a hand moving. It was barely visible as some empty boxes were laying around. He grabbed a couple of boxes out of the way and saw the man.

His face was covered in dried blood and he weakly whispered, "Can you help me, kind sir?"

Donovan removed the other boxes that covered him and checked out his injuries. He immediately began to call for an ambulance but the man told him 'no.' Donovan said okay and called out to the kitchen staff. They were more than happy to give the poor man some towels and the medical supplies they had on hand. The server who he saw earlier, started to clean his facial wounds and bandaged him up. He said he was okay but Donovan insisted on taking him back to the inn. He was going to get him cleaned up thoroughly, and hopefully, find out who he was and if he was connected to Weldon or Amber.

Donovan called an Uber and after getting the man into the car, he texted William to let him know so he could get a wheelchair from the inn and help get him into his room. He didn't want to call attention to the man; he was in such poor shape. William was waiting and had a blanket to put over him. They lifted him out of the car and into the chair. They quickly got past the front desk and then into the elevator. After getting him in the room, they cleaned him up as best they could. Donovan called down for room service while William went to a nearby clothing store. The man had been through a lot and they were going to take care of him.

After he ate, Donovan asked him if he felt well enough to take a bath. He nodded his head and afterward, Donovan hoped he would be able to get him to talk. Katelyn called while the man was bathing and she didn't have any news to report. He told her he would call her back. She didn't know about the man and he wanted to wait and see what he could find out.

William got back just as the man was getting ready to use Donovan's robe that was hanging on a hook in the bathroom. Luckily, William selected the right size clothing and the man must have felt better and muttered he needed to go back.

"Oh no, you're not going anywhere!" Donovan was not letting him out of his sight.

"You need to rest and get better," William added.

"Okay, one night," he whispered. "You both are too kind."

Donovan couldn't hold off any longer. He had to find out who he was. "Can you tell us your name?"

The man ignored the question and William said, "Maybe later he'll feel like talking."

Donovan was going crazy inside. Then he remembered the man's dirty clothing was probably still lying on the bathroom floor. He said, "Okay, I understand," and then walked into the bathroom to look inside his clothing.

He was going to have to throw everything in the outside dumpster. I never saw or smelled anything so bad, he thought. Then he found what he was looking for - his wallet. There was a driver's license on top. No, it can't be! The license belonged to Weldon Hopper. How did this man get Weldon's wallet?

Was he a thief? Then it dawned on him. The clue from the book said the man was kind. Since the man never looked at them and always kept his head down, Donovan never got a good look at him. Could it really be Weldon? Was he alive? If not, how did this poor man get his wallet? He walked out holding the wallet. The man took one look and realized what he had found.

"Weldon, is it really you?" he asked.

William looked at Donovan like he was out of his mind. The man looked up and said, "It's about time!"

Donovan and William were in shock. "What is going on? Why are you living on the streets and poor Amber is sitting in prison for your murder?" Donovan was outraged that Weldon would pull such a stunt.

"Calm down, Donovan. Let me explain everything."

They sat down at the table and wanted him to fill them in on everything. He started at the beginning. He and Amber were working on a book but it was nowhere near finished. Amber didn't realize he was working on a book of his own about events currently taking place in his life in case anything happened to him. She was like a daughter to him and he didn't want to worry her. When he found out she was arrested and charged with his murder, he had to go undercover and try to find out who was behind it.

William stopped him and said, "But they took someone out in a body bag that day claiming it was you."

"Yes, and that's where the story gets really strange. I don't know who was in the bag, and notice, nothing more has been said about my death in the papers."

"After it happened, the papers printed a couple of stories about Amber and you having an affair and she killed you when she found out you were cheating on her."

"I don't know where they got that idea. Probably from that nosy neighbor who lives next door. I asked the private investigator to get her name cleared but he keeps saying he almost has her out."

"What do you know about the guy they found in your wine room?"

"That is probably the man who has been claiming to be a long, lost brother of mine. The private investigator I hired was going to let him out after the cops left. I only wanted to scare him away."

"Is Brad the name of your private investigator?"

"Yes, and I never knew he was the same one that was hired by my imposter of a long, lost brother until recently when things weren't being done I was paying him for."

Before they went any further, they wanted to bring Katelyn and Ellen along with Drew and Michelle into the loop. It was almost time for the afternoon meeting and they could all sit down and see what they could come up with.

William called Katelyn and asked if she and Ellen could come to Donovan's room for the four o'clock meeting while Donovan contacted Michelle and Drew. They all agreed and Weldon told Drew and Michelle over the phone about the beating he took early this morning.

"I thought no one would ever find me. I'm so thankful you looked for me, Donovan. I can't thank you enough."

They agreed to keep it to themselves and not worry Ellen or Katelyn about what happened.

At three forty-five, Katelyn and Ellen knocked on Donovan's door. It was probably a good thing they were early as they were in for a huge shock. When they entered the room and found Weldon, they were overwhelmed. They both hugged him and his poorly bruised body was aching but he didn't care. His friends were there and he was happy to see them. They waited until four o'clock for Michelle and Drew. Weldon had a lot of explaining to do and he was ready. He texted Brad and asked him to meet him in the parking lot of the inn at six o'clock.

Michelle and Drew came in together. Drew looked at Weldon and knew who he was. Confused, he couldn't understand how he could be alive when the police reported him dead and Amber being the killer. Weldon told them everything he knew. He said he detected a bad cop but didn't know who it was. Drew said he and Stan were the arresting officers but they did nothing with the body that was found. He was thinking back to the day of the arrest. There were a lot of officers and the neighbors were there along with the new coroner. Who was in the body bag? Drew was going to find out.

Next, they discussed deep throat. "Who is deep throat?" Weldon asked.

"He's the person who's leaving notes on our doors."

"Did he sound like this: "Gentlemen, if you want to find out what happened to Weldon Hopper…"

"That was you! Why didn't you tell us?" William asked.

"To be honest, I was afraid I'd scare you all off before we figured out who was behind all of this. I didn't know if I could trust any police officers, I'm sorry, Drew, and secondly, the private investigator I hired wasn't doing his job but I was in no position to fire him and hire another one since everyone thought I was dead. And," he added, "the first attorney you hired had a big mouth for an assistant."

"You heard about that, Weldon?" Katelyn asked.

"Yes, I went into the diner when I saw you both inside. I overheard your conversation with that woman. It was difficult to know who I could trust besides my friends."

"I'm sorry you went through so much. Now, how soon can we get Amber out of prison?" Donovan hated seeing her suffer.

"Well, I think we need to find out what's going on down at the precinct. If there's a bad cop, I have to find out. Let's hang in there a couple more days. In the meantime, we need to find out about your private investigator. I'll run a check on him. Next, I have to go to the hospital to check on your so-called long, lost brother," Drew said.

"I'd like to join you," Weldon advised. "It should be an enjoyable visit," he said with a laugh.

"It looks like you'll have your hands full," Michelle said looking over at Drew.

"Yes, but it'll be worth it to get Amber out of prison and get this mess cleared up."

Weldon looked at his watch and saw it was five-thirty. He told them he was meeting Brad in the parking lot at six o'clock. "Perfect," Drew commented, "I'll be watching."

He gave Weldon his cell phone number and he was going to call it before his meeting. Drew wanted Weldon to find out as much as he could.

At six o'clock, Brad walked out of the inn and saw Weldon sitting on a bench. He waved and Brad walked over. "How's it going?" he asked Weldon.

"Just a little run-in with someone trying to beat me up this morning, but other than that, I'm okay."

"Gee Weldon, are you sure about that?"

Drew was sitting in his car and was taking a few photos. Weldon had given him Brad's last name and he wanted to run a check on him.

"Yes, just a couple of bruises here and there," Weldon replied.

"Did you ever get that man claiming to be my brother out of my house?" he asked.

"Uh, yeah, sure, why?"

"I'm asking because I'm paying you to do a job and want to know everything is being taken care of."

"Sure, I understand."

"How soon is Amber going to be released?"

"Well, the cops are still stalling but I'm trying to get her out. I'll keep on them."

"Who are you working with down there?" Weldon asked.

He was hoping to get the name of the bad cop. "It's a new guy by the name of Reynolds. He said he'd take care of everything."

Drew was perplexed. That was the name of the sergeant. He didn't know of any new guy named Reynolds. Then it dawned on him. The sergeant's nephew filled in for Ed while he was on vacation. Could it be him? He was anxious to find out. Weldon pressed on.

"I don't believe I know that guy. What did you say his first name was?"

"I believe it's Joe."

"Okay, well see what you can find out about the investigation. Do you know where the cops put my computer and other things they took out of my house?"

"I'm working on finding out. I'll check with Joe tomorrow."

"Are you able to contact him now?" Weldon asked.

"I'll try but he may be out on a call."

"I understand but I'd appreciate knowing where my things are. It'll make me feel better knowing they are safe."

"Okay, and when Brad dialed the number, Weldon moved his arm directly toward Brad and knocked his phone out of his hand. He looked down and saw that Brad had not placed a call.

"Brad, what's going on? You aren't calling anyone? I want answers and I want them now, young man!"

"I should have slapped you harder when I had the chance," Brad hollered.

Upon hearing that, Drew jumped out of his car and ran over to them. As Drew read him his rights, he handcuffed him and called in for a patrol car. He was going to enjoy taking his statement. But he didn't want to put him in jail until they discovered who the person was he was working with at the precinct.

The next day, Drew walked into the jail-holding cell where Brad was. It wasn't reported that he was arrested last night. "You can make this easy or hard," Drew began as he took out a form to begin taking down his statement.

"What are you talking about?" Brad asked.

"Well, let's see, I can get you for mugging, having a man locked up for days in a vacant house, and for your involvement in framing Amber Jenkins."

"Wait a minute, I didn't do all of those things!"

"Okay, tell me what you know and maybe we can work out a deal with the District Attorney."

Upon hearing that, Brad spilled everything he knew. The cop he was working with was Joe Reynolds, nephew of the sergeant. When Joe realized his uncle wasn't going to help him out by getting him into the academy, he decided to work with Brad and get some of Weldon's wealth. It seemed that the long-lost brother who showed up promised them fifty thousand dollars each for faking Weldon's death and framing Amber. The body bag that was carried out sadly contained the remains of a homeless person who had passed away in a warehouse fire. Joe had the body removed from the morgue and placed it at Weldon's. Due to the condition of the body, no one was the wiser. The person who said they saw Amber enter Weldon's home was Brad himself. He was wearing a wig, sunglasses and had jeans and an oversized long coat on.

The long, lost brother decided not to pay them after they followed through with all of his requests. They got mad and locked him up in the wine room. As far as the computer and other items, Joe wanted to remove them from Weldon's house in case there was any incriminating information stored on them. Everything was later removed from the property room at the precinct and returned to his home.

"Well, this is quite a tale," Drew remarked.

"It's the truth, and I'm not proud of what I did," Brad replied.

"Are you still in contact with Joe Reynolds?"

"Yes, he's been bugging me about getting the money from Carl."

"Is that the name of the guy claiming to be Weldon's brother?"

"Yes, his name is Carl Walters."

"Okay, I'll need you to call Joe and set up a meeting. Remember, you will be wired, and for me to keep my promise about talking to the District Attorney on your behalf, you have to cooperate."

"I understand. I want to make things right."

Drew was glad it wasn't a bad cop that worked at the precinct who was responsible for what happened. Although, it didn't make him feel good to know it was the sergeant's nephew. He felt bad and knew he was going to take it hard.

The sting was set up for two o'clock the next day. Brad called Joe and told him that he finally got the payoff from Carl. They were going to meet at the roadside rest outside of town. Drew informed Michelle of everything he had learned and of the meeting between Brad and Joe. He couldn't tell the sergeant but Stan was going to be there along with some unmarked patrol cars in the nearby vicinity.

When Brad saw Joe pull up, he waved him over. Joe got out of the car and Brad sat down on a bench. Joe joined him as they made a little small talk before they got into talking about what they did. "So old Carl finally decided to give us our share?" Joe asked.

"Yeah, I told him I was going to rat him out if he didn't pay up."

Joe chuckled and said, "What about the other old guy, Weldon? Is he still doing the disappearing act?"

"Well, he didn't come out of hiding yet, that I know of. That dame is still in jail the last I heard."

"Wow, I do feel sorry for her. She didn't do anything, and to top it off, the guy's not even dead!"

"I know, did you ever find anything on Weldon's computer that would tie us to any of this?" Brad asked.

"Naw, I had it taken back to his house after I checked it out. Just some boring books he was writing, nothing about us."

"That's good," Brad replied.

"Well, I gotta get going. Where's my share of the cash at?"

Brad got up and the plan was that as soon as he handed the money over to Joe, Drew and the other officers were going to pull in and arrest him. Drew told the officers that it was real cash so they had to make sure they retrieved it.

Brad opened his trunk and his shirt button popped open. Joe saw the wire and immediately knew he was set up. He pulled out a gun from underneath his jacket and was getting ready to aim it at Brad when Drew gave the command for the patrol cars to move in and circle around them. They had all the evidence they needed.

At the police station, word circulated pretty fast about the sergeant's nephew. The Chief of Police stopped by and told Sergeant Reynolds he was going on an unpaid administrative leave, effective immediately. The department needed to do a thorough investigation as to why the sergeant's nephew worked for a week in the precinct. They didn't know if the sergeant was involved in any way.

Michelle had all the proof she needed to get Amber released from jail. Carl was released from the hospital and traded his hospital bed in for a jail cot. The District Attorney was going to go a little easy on Brad since he cooperated and helped to bring down Carl and Joe. And best of all, Weldon was alive and well.

Before everyone left to go home, Weldon and Amber hosted everyone to a celebratory dinner. They invited their new friends, Michelle and Drew, and of course, all of their author friends, as well as Abby. Weldon didn't want to have it at his home since he felt his house was no longer a place where he wanted to live. Ellen understood as she thought about her own home and knew the upcoming trip would do them all good. It was only two weeks away before they were off on the murder mystery cruise.

"I can't wait to see what kind of mystery we're in for this time," William commented.

"Anything will be better than sitting in a jail cell," Amber said jokingly.

"Or living on the street day in, day out," Weldon added.

Donovan and Ellen looked at each other and laughed. "Boy, do we have our very own mystery to fill you in on, but that's for another time!" she remarked. "What matters most is we're all safe now and going to have an enjoyable cruise involving a fictional mystery this time."

Ellen turned to Donovan, who hadn't mentioned Brigitte in a while. "Well, I guess you'll be excited to see your mademoiselle," she said with a smile.

"Uh, about Brigitte, she won't be accompanying me on the cruise."

"I'm sorry to hear that," William responded. "We looked forward to meeting her."

"Well, I think when you're on vacation, especially in a country like France, it's easy to fall in love with someone. But when you return home, things are different and you grow apart. I think I'll stick to girls closer to home from now on," he said with a grin.

Weldon stood to thank everyone for helping to solve another real-life mystery he was involved in. "Dear friends, I want you to know how much I appreciate all of you. I know it's not easy putting up with a grumpy old man, but I do value all of your friendships. If you wouldn't have been there for Amber and me, I'm not sure what would have happened to us. Thank you for not giving up and I guess the next time I see you, we'll all be cruising!"

"It's too bad Drew and Michelle won't be joining us," Katelyn said sadly. "They were a big part of helping to solve the mystery."

Weldon looked over and at her and said, "Don't worry, my dear. I already checked with the Mystery Writers Association, and if they're available to go, I got them covered."

Drew looked at Weldon and said, "I have a lot of extra vacation time stored up. If you're sure, I'd love to join all of you."

Michelle said, "I would love to go too!"

Ellen was so happy they would be joining them. "I guess that solves it. We'll all be together again! Get packed and see you in two weeks!"

Michelle looked over at Abby and said, "Okay, you can have your story now."

Abby got up and went over to hug Weldon and Amber. She told them she was glad they were okay and can't wait to interview them on her show.

Weldon put his hands up in the air and said, "Why me?"

They all laughed and she said she was just kidding. Katelyn wondered what made her change her mind. Weldon was thankful to have friends that looked out for him and he knew Abby was going to get her interview with them one way or the other.

To be Continued Sailing through the Bermuda Triangle

Made in United States
Orlando, FL
15 October 2022

23447848R00104